Ana María Reyes Does Not Live in a Castle

HILDA EUNICE BURGOS

TU BOOKS

AN IMPRINT OF LEE & LOW BOOKS INC.
NEW YORK

Copyright © 2018 by Hilda Eunice Burgos
Jacket illustration copyright © 2018 by Lissy Marlin

TU BOOKS
an imprint of LEE & LOW BOOKS Inc.
95 Madison Avenue, New York, NY 10016
leeandlow.com

Manufactured in the United States of America by Worzalla Publishing Company

FSC
www.fsc.org
MIX
Paper from
responsible sources
FSC® C002589

Edited by Cheryl Klein
Book design by Neil Swaab
Typesetting by ElfElm Publishing
Book production by The Kids at Our House
The text is set in Dante MT Pro
with display fonts in Homeward Bound, Buntaro, and Appelstroop
Vector illustration by Leeva de Mama / Shutterstock.com

10 9 8 7 6 5 4 3 2 1
First Edition

Library of Congress Cataloging-in-Publication Data
Names: Burgos, Hilda Eunice, author.
Title: Ana María Reyes does not live in a castle / Hilda Eunice Burgos.
Description: First edition. | New York : Tu Books, an imprint of Lee & Low Books Inc., [2018] |
Summary: "With a new sibling (her fourth) on the way and a big piano recital on the horizon, Dominican-American Ana María Reyes tries to win a scholarship to a New York City private school" -- Provided by publisher. |
Identifiers: LCCN 2018022776 (print) | LCCN 2018029111 (ebook) | ISBN 9781620143643 (mobi)
ISBN 9781620143636 (epub) | ISBN 9781620143629 (hardcover : alk. paper)
Subjects: | CYAC: Family life--New York (State)--New York--Fiction. |
Dominican Americans--Fiction. | Ability--Fiction. | Scholarships--Fiction. |
Bronx (New York, N.Y.)--Fiction.
Classification: LCC PZ7.1.B875 (ebook) | LCC PZ7.1.B875 An 2018 (print) | DDC [Fic]--dc23
LC record available at https://lccn.loc.gov/2018022776

For my parents,
who will always be royalty in my book

CAST OF CHARACTERS

The Reyes Family

Anamay (Ana María): eleven years old

Gracie (Altagracia): Anamay's thirteen-year-old sister

Rosie (Rosalba): Anamay's six-year-old sister

Connie (Consuelo): Anamay's three-year-old sister

Mami (Mercedes "Mecho" Castillo de Reyes): Anamay's mother

Papi (Gustavo "Tavito" Reyes): Anamay's father

Friends and Family in New York City

Abuelita: Anamay's grandmother, Mami's mother

Tío Lalo: Mami's brother

Claudia: Anamay's best friend

Ruben Rivera: Anamay's friend

Doña Dulce Sánchez: Anamay's piano teacher

Sarita Gómez: Gracie's classmate and Doña Dulce's star piano
student

Lucy: Sarita's sister

Chichi, Lydia, and Millie: Mami's friends

Pedro, Vicky, and Rebecca: Gracie's friends

Friends and Family in the Dominican Republic

Tía Nona: Mami's younger sister

Juan Miguel: Tía Nona's fiancé/husband

Tía Chea: Mami's older sister

Tío Pepe: Tía Chea's husband

Pepito, Juancito, and Muñeca: Tía Chea's children

Tío Rogelio and Tío Marcos: Papi's brothers

Clarisa ("Cosita"): Tía Nona's maid

Chapter 1

GRACIE SAID MAMI WAS RIGHT TO slap me. She thought I deserved it for what I said. But there were things my sister didn't know about. Like the conversation I had just had with our parents.

"Look what Mr. Briller gave me!" I told them when I got home from school that day in June. I should have known something fishy was going on because Papi wasn't at work. But I didn't ask, because I was glad he was home. He would appreciate the good news I'd gotten from my sixth-grade counselor. "The Eleanor School is offering merit scholarships for the first time in forever, and Mr. Briller thinks I can get one! I just have to take a test in October and fill out this application." I showed them the packet.

Education means everything to my parents. So the chance to have their daughter go to a top-notch private school for not too much money would be thrilling to them, right? Wrong. They glanced at each other with worried faces.

1

Mami twisted her fingers around like a shy kid about to give an oral report. Papi cleared his throat.

"Ana María," he said, "that's a very expensive school. And in eighth grade, you can take the test for Bronx Science." That was the fancy public high school where a lot of super smart kids in New York City went. Since my neighborhood—Washington Heights—is close to the Bronx, Science was my parents' dream school for their kids.

"But it's a scholarship," I said. "So Eleanor won't be that expensive. And there's no guarantee that I'll get into Science. Gracie didn't."

My parents looked at each other again. I knew what they were thinking: Gracie never had a shot at Science because she wasn't a great student. Unlike me. But they would never say that out loud, because they liked to pretend their four daughters were identical in every way: equally smart, talented, beautiful, sweet, and so on.

"Well . . ." Papi said. "That doesn't mean anything. I think you definitely have a good chance."

"But I have a chance at the Eleanor School right now. Don't you want me to get a good education?"

"Of course we do, *mija*," Mami said. "And you'll get one, just like your sister, even though she's not going to Science."

My face started to grow warm. "Little Bethlehem High School is nowhere near as good as Eleanor. Not a single member of their graduating class last year went on to an Ivy League school. And look at all that Eleanor has to offer." I opened the shiny brochure and stood between my parents so they could see the photos of the sprawling green campus, the ginormous science lab with room for all the students to spread out, the happy-looking kids playing brand-new instruments on a polished stage.

Papi sighed. "The Eleanor School costs six times more than Little Bethlehem," he said. "We know that a good education is important to you, and we're very proud of you, but we just can't afford a place like that."

"What if I get a full scholarship?"

My parents' eyes met again, and they nodded at the same time. "Of course," Mami said. "We would be thrilled if that happened."

"But don't get your hopes up," Papi said. "After all, we still have to save up for college, and not just for you. We have to think of your sisters too."

I nodded. Of course I understood. My friend Claudia went to the Eleanor School, and she always talked about how wonderful it was. The caring teachers, the cool field trips, all the different foreign languages offered. Even Latin, which would help with my SATs. But Claudia was an only child. Plus, both her parents made a lot of money. They graduated from Columbia Law School with my dad, which is how they all became friends. But Papi didn't go on to a fancy law firm like they did. He got his dream job at a place that helps people for free.

"So I can take the scholarship exam, right?" I asked.

"Of course," Papi said.

"Well," Mami said to Papi. "Maybe now is a good time for our family meeting."

Papi nodded. "Ana María, please go get Altagracia, Rosalba, and Consuelo."

I walked down the hall to the bedroom I shared with Gracie and our six-year-old sister, Rosie. They were on the floor playing with Connie and her dolls. Even though she was only three, Connie could be pretty bossy. "No, no, no!" she was saying to Gracie as I walked in. "You're the teacher and I'm the mom."

"Well, who am I?" Rosie looked confused.

"Family meeting, guys," I said.

Gracie rolled her eyes. Ever since she turned thirteen, that was her favorite thing to do. "Now what?"

I shrugged. The four of us walked down the hall single file.

"Okay, is everyone here?" Papi put his arm around Mami's shoulder and stood in front of us kids with a big smile on his face.

"We know how much you girls would like to have a brother someday," Mami said. "And now that just might happen!"

She and Papi giggled, and I started to get a bad feeling in my stomach.

"The new baby will be here in December, near Christmas," Papi said.

"Oh . . ." Gracie looked at me, and I knew right away she wasn't happy. "That's . . . great."

I could not believe this. I didn't need my own room or fancy designer clothes. It didn't bother me that we each got only two gifts at Christmas. And I understood that my parents didn't always have time to watch me win spelling bees and science fairs. But I really, really wanted—no, needed—a good education. And I might not be able to get one because my parents had too many kids. That was surely why they didn't want to pay anything for the Eleanor School.

"Where's the baby gonna sleep?" Connie asked. She wanted to sleep in my parents' room forever.

"In your crib," I said. "And you'll be sleeping on the floor."

"Ana María, you know that's not true," Papi said. "Consuelo, we'll make sleeping arrangements when the time gets closer."

"I don't remember saying I wanted a brother." Rosie tapped her chin.

"Ay, Rosalba." Gracie coughed out a fake laugh and rubbed Rosie's shoulders. "Kids," she said to Mami and Papi. "They have such poor memories sometimes."

"There's nothing wrong with her memory," I said. Now I was really mad. "None of us wants a brother or another sister. Why do you have to have so many kids anyway? You're too old to be walking around pregnant. This is embarrassing!"

That's when Mami slapped me.

* * *

The moments after the slap felt like they were happening to someone else and I was just watching. I held my hand up to my left cheek. Mami covered her face, burst into tears, and ran down the hall to her bedroom. Gracie gasped. Papi gave me this look, like he was appalled at my very existence, then followed after Mami. Connie scrunched up her face and cried the way she always does whenever she sees tears in someone else's eyes, and Rosie stroked Connie's head and told her everything would be okay.

"You deserved that!" Gracie said to me, her nostrils flaring.

"That's easy for you to say," I said. "You've never been hit before in your life!"

"Duh," Gracie said. "Neither had you until right now."

I put my chin in the air. "Well, I guess we're different now."

"You're crazy," Gracie said. "That's nothing to be proud of."

"You're not happy about this new baby either," I said. "But you're too much of a phony to say anything."

"This has nothing to do with being phony! It's about being polite and, more importantly, being nice to your mother!" Gracie stomped down the hall and into our bedroom. Rosie and Connie trotted after her. The door shut with a thud, keeping me out.

I stood there and looked at the empty hallway, then I

sat on the piano bench with my back to the piano, facing the living room. Had I done something wrong? I was just being honest. And why would Mami want a son anyway? Didn't she see that might hurt our feelings? Plus, where in the world would this new kid fit? We weren't a bunch of socks my parents could squish into a drawer. I took off my glasses and rubbed the lenses with the edge of my T-shirt until all the smudges were gone. Then I put my glasses back on and stared at the sharp creases Mami had ironed into my pink cotton pants.

I remembered the first time I walked into this apartment, when I was three years old. I actually thought this place was huge back then. It was still empty, and it seemed as big as a castle. The powder-blue carpet was brand new and springy underneath my feet, and I ran straight through the living room to the wall of windows. From up here on the twelfth floor, the cars looked like toys, and the people would have fit into my hands.

Gracie lay down on the floor of our bedroom and moved her arms and legs back and forth, making snow angels on the pink rug. Mami and Papi took me to their bedroom, which had a door leading to a cement terrace with a high iron fence all around it. We went out to the terrace and Mami held my hand tightly. When I took a step toward the fence, she pulled me back. "I don't want you to fall over," she said. Then she showed me the bathroom, full of room to move around. I thought we lived in a mansion.

I was wrong. Now we can't look out the windows because of Mami's jungle of plants. The bathroom is stuffed with hair products, magazines, and laundry hampers, and my sisters and I are so crammed into our tiny bedroom, there isn't even room for a bookshelf. And my parents wanted to squeeze another person in here? I was getting angry again. I got up and opened the piano bench. Practicing would calm me down. It always did.

As I sat back down I accidentally knocked over one of the photos on top of the piano. It was the one of Papi's mother, who I never got a chance to meet before she died three years ago. Papi used to go to the Dominican Republic to visit her every year. I remembered one time, when I was five, he brought home some guava-and-milk candy packed among his clothes. The wrapping must have come loose, because when he opened the suitcase, ants swarmed all around. Mami and Papi quickly dragged the suitcase into the bathtub. Mami grabbed all the clothes and took them to the laundry room in the basement. Papi threw the food out in the trash chute in the hallway outside our apartment. And they scrubbed the suitcase clean. But I still couldn't get those ants out of my mind. I woke Mami up three times in the middle of the night because I felt like ants were crawling all over my body. First she scrubbed me down with a washcloth and helped me put on different pajamas. Then she changed my sheets. Finally she took me into her bed and let me sleep with her. All for imaginary insects.

"I guess Mami's not so bad," I said to my grandmother's picture. "And I definitely shouldn't have called her old. Old people hate that." I put the photo down and headed toward my parents' bedroom. I was a little nervous about apologizing to Mami. She always forgave us no matter what we did, but she also never got upset enough to hit us. So she was obviously super mad today. I lifted my hand to her closed door and took a deep breath before knocking.

Papi opened the door and nodded when he saw me. Then he left the room so I could be alone with Mami. She was sitting on the edge of the bed, still sniffling a little.

"I'm sorry, Mami," I said. She looked so sad and I felt like an awful person for hurting her feelings. "You're not old, and you're not embarrassing. I'm proud that you're my mother." I really meant that, but I didn't know if she would believe me.

Mami patted the bed beside her. "Come, sit down." She stroked the hair above my ear, then curled the bottom of my braid with her finger. "Anamay, I'm so sorry I hit you. I shouldn't have lost my temper like that."

"That's okay," I said. "It didn't really hurt that much." Which was actually true.

"You know your father and I will always love you and your sisters very much. That's the great thing about a family. Love is multiplied when there are more people, not divided."

I stared at my fingernails.

"You do know that, right?" Mami said.

I nodded. I did not look up. Math was my best subject at school, and Mami's calculations didn't sound right to me.

Mami waited a little bit before she spoke again. "Tell me what's bothering you."

I shrugged. My glasses were sliding down my nose, so I pushed them back up with one finger. Mami was still waiting. She wasn't going to leave me alone until I said something. But I couldn't tell her the truth. If I said I didn't think she loved me as much as my sisters, and that a new baby would make that even worse, she might admit I was right. And I didn't want to hear that. "I just really want to go to the Eleanor School," I said. "Plus, this place is so small. When Connie grows out of the crib, there'll be four of us in one room. And where will this last kid fit?"

"*Ay*, Anamay, you worry too much. We'll figure out a way." She smiled a little. "And remember, we are the Reyes! Wherever we live is our castle."

Mami's family's last name is Castillo, and Papi's last name is Reyes. In the Dominican Republic, where both my parents were born, when a woman gets married, she keeps her name, adds an "of" in Spanish, or *de*, and then follows it with her husband's name. So Mami is a Castillo de Reyes, which means "castle of kings" in Spanish. And that's how my parents described our home. A castle filled with royalty: our Reyes family.

"Yeah, I know," I said. "Our castle of kings."

Mami pulled me toward her for a hug. She didn't know I was just being polite.

Chapter 2

THE NEXT DAY I WENT TO my piano lesson, as I did every Tuesday after school. My piano teacher, Doña Dulce Sánchez, lived two blocks from my school, in the opposite direction from my house. Her building only had six floors, and the entryway was dark and smelled like dirty wet towels. The elevator broke down a lot, but even when it worked, it was super slow so I didn't bother waiting for it. Doña Dulce did not like it when a student arrived late.

"I can't believe that woman's name is Dulce," Gracie said before she quit taking lessons. "There's nothing sweet about her."

Doña Dulce was definitely tough, and she noticed when you hadn't practiced. One time she made Gracie play one scale over and over again for her entire lesson. "And that's how you practice," Doña Dulce said when the hour was up. Gracie was in tears. She told Mami and Papi that she refused to be mistreated anymore, so they let her quit. I tried to talk her out of it, but she wouldn't listen to me. Now, after six years of lessons, I could say that, even though she was demanding, Doña Dulce was a really great teacher. In fact, she was probably great *because* she was demanding. And it's a wonderful feeling when you finally get a piece right and you hear that beautiful music flowing from your fingers.

As I stood outside the apartment, I could hear Sarita Gómez playing inside. Sarita lived on the sixth floor of Doña Dulce's building. Her family didn't have a piano, so she came over every day after school to practice on Doña Dulce's second piano. It was in the front bedroom, the one that Doña Dulce's son used to live in before he joined the Marines and moved away.

Doña Dulce's husband answered the door when I knocked. He stepped to the side so I could squeeze past him into the apartment. I was a little early, so I stopped to listen to Sarita play. Whenever Sarita played I held my breath, because I felt like I'd miss something if I did anything other than just listen. Her playing was so beautiful. Gracie always said Sarita had a special gift, and we couldn't expect to ever be that good, but I wasn't going to give up that easily. I admired Sarita's hard work, and she inspired me to work hard too.

Mr. Sánchez had stopped to listen as well. When Sarita paused, he smiled at me and clicked shut all seven of the locks on the door. "Dulce's waiting for you," he said.

I walked down the hallway to the living room. Doña Dulce was not alone. As I came into the room, three people dressed in business suits stood up from the plastic-covered sofa where they had been cramped together—one young woman and two gray-haired men. My teacher shuffled toward me and took my arm. "This is Ana María, one of my best students," she said.

"*Hola*, Ana María," the woman said. "Do you speak English?"

"Of course," I said. I squinted at her, then remembered that Gracie always said that was my are-you-an-idiot look, so I quickly opened my eyes wide.

"Oh, wonderful!" one of the men said. "My name is Alan Flynn, and these are my colleagues Ms. Alonzo and Mr. Smith. We're from the Piano Teachers' Association."

This was weird. Every year Doña Dulce took her students downtown to be tested by the Piano Teachers' Association. We each brought a list of about ten pieces we had memorized, and the association judge picked a few for us to play. Doña Dulce said this was how we knew we were really learning, and not just enough to satisfy her. This past year I scored a 92, and Sarita got a 99, even though she probably deserved a 100.

"The testers have been so impressed with the quality of Mrs. Sánchez's students that we have invited her to bring two performers to our Winter Showcase. Are you familiar with the Winter Showcase?" I shook my head, and Mr. Flynn continued, "We cosponsor it with the Eleanor School, and top piano students from all over the city perform at Lincoln Center."

The Eleanor School! Would the scholarship people come to the showcase? Could this help me get a full ride?

"So," Mr. Flynn said, "we will observe your lesson today and later select the two students who will perform."

"Okay," I said. I just stood there, not sure what to do next. I couldn't stop thinking about the possibility of that scholarship.

"Come, come, sit down." Doña Dulce ushered me onto the piano bench. She took her usual seat in the chair beside me. The plastic on the couch grunted when the three visitors sat back down. "Let's start with Schumann. 'The Happy Farmer.'"

I was relieved to hear that. When I first learned to play "The Happy Farmer," I struggled with some of the chords, but not anymore. I started loudly with my left hand, softly with the right. My fingers bounced on the keys, hitting the right notes on tempo, switching the dynamics at the correct moments, ending with a soft, slow chord. By the time I finished, I had forgotten all about the Piano Teachers' Association people. But then I heard papers rustling and whispered voices, and, right away, I remembered. "Very well executed staccato," one man murmured. "Great rhythm," the woman said. I looked at Doña Dulce without turning my head. She was looking at me too. We both smiled.

The rest of the lesson went by quickly. Every time I stopped playing, I heard positive comments from the association people. Then I would sit up a little taller and play a little louder for the next piece. Not to brag, but by the time I played my last piece, I probably sounded like Sarita. Doña Dulce also had me play a few scales and arpeggios to show that I had the basics down.

When my hour was over, I stood up. I wondered if I should just leave or turn around and say goodbye.

"It was very nice to meet you, Ann Marie," Mr. Flynn said. He held his arm out and shook my hand just like a grown-up.

"Ana María," I said.

He looked puzzled.

"My name. It's Ana María, not Ann Marie."

Mr. Flynn lifted his chin, frowned, and said, "Ohhh." He looked a little annoyed.

Maybe I shouldn't have said that, I thought. *Maybe I won't get picked now.*

Sarita was in the hallway waiting to come into the living room when I left. We looked at each other and smiled. "You sounded great," she whispered to me.

"Thanks." I squeezed past her and headed toward the door. Then I turned around and said, "Good luck, Sarita." She smiled and gave me a little wave before going into the living room.

Of course she didn't need any luck. She was definitely going to Lincoln Center. Why did she have to play for them right after me? They would never remember me now.

Chapter 3

CALLED CLAUDIA AS SOON AS I got home from my lesson. She shrieked when I told her about the Winter Showcase. "This is sooo exciting!" she said. "I've seen the showcase, and the kids were really good, just like you!"

I smiled. My friend was so sweet, but was I really as good as those kids? "Do you think this might help me get a scholarship?" I asked.

"Oh, definitely. Eleanor's head of school always goes to that, and she knows it's a big deal to be picked to perform. Plus she loves to brag about her students, so she wants kids who do cool stuff like play at Lincoln Center. And then we'll be at the same school!" She squealed so loudly I had to hold the phone away from my ear. I was excited too, but I had to admit that it didn't take much to get Claudia worked up. She even went crazy when I told her about the new baby. "Also, the performers get really dressed up. The girls wear fancy gowns like they're going to a ball, and the boys wear tuxedos. It's like playing in a real orchestra or something."

Hmm, I wasn't sure about that. I didn't have any ballroom gowns. But it didn't make sense to worry about that just yet. I didn't even know if I was going.

"And then when you get to Eleanor, the music director will beg you to be in the orchestra," Claudia said. She went on and on about the classes we would take together at Eleanor and the extracurricular activities we would join. She loved to sing, so she was in the choir. "Sometimes the jazz band uses singers, so I'm going to try out for that, and I know they'll need a piano player, so you should audition too. Oh, I'm so excited!" She shrieked again. I laughed as we said goodbye, then I hung up the phone and went to join Mami and my sisters in the kitchen.

Abuelita had arrived while I was on the phone. She was sitting at the dining table, sideways in her chair, her hands folded over her lap, watching Mami scurry about in the kitchen. Rosie stood on her stool in front of the sink, washing a bowl of lettuce. Gracie sat at the table across from Abuelita. She was embroidering flowers onto a T-shirt for Connie, who sat next to her with a fistful of thread: red, pink, yellow, green, blue, and orange. She handed a pink strand to Gracie.

"Garlic has such a strong smell; it'll stay on your hands forever," Abuelita was saying when I walked up to her. I bent down and kissed her cheek. The smell of her perfume made my eyes water a little. Abuelita was even more dressed up than usual, with pearls and a fancy purple dress.

"*Bendición*, Abuelita," I said.

"*Que Dios te bendiga, mi amor.*" Abuelita gave me her blessing. Then she turned back to Mami. "You should wear some rubber gloves, *mija.*"

Mami nodded as she mashed the garlic in the mortar with a pestle. She scooped the mush out with her bare fingers and lathered it onto the chicken right before she put it in the oven. "How was your lesson?" she asked me.

I told her about the Winter Showcase and how it might help me get a scholarship.

"You know Sarita's going," Gracie said without looking up from her embroidery. "But you might get the second spot."

"Claudia says the performers wear fancy gowns and tuxedos," I said.

"Oh!" Gracie put the T-shirt down and looked at Mami. "I can make a dress for Anamay to wear to Lincoln Center!"

"What? No, I'm not wearing one of your sewing experiments!"

"Actually, that's a good idea," Mami said. "Of course, the material for a fancy dress is harder to work with, so I'll help. But we can make something much nicer than we could afford from a store."

"Can't we buy a regular dress like everybody else?" I said. "*If* I go, of course." I didn't want to get my hopes up, just in case.

"Don't worry, Anamay," Abuelita said. "You know your mother is a wonderful seamstress."

"Yeah, I know *she* is."

Gracie gave me the evil eye. I glared right back at her.

"You must be exhausted, Mecho!" Abuelita said to Mami. "Standing over a hot stove in your condition! Here, let me help you." She stood up.

"No, Mamá, I'm fine. Anamay will help."

Ugh, cooking. That was Rosie's thing, not mine. But I didn't have any homework, so I could help out. "Sure," I said. "What do you need?"

Mami handed me some tomatoes and cucumbers and asked me to cut them up to add to the salad. "Rosita, keep an eye on the rice and let me know when the water cooks out." She sat down next to Abuelita to peel a bunch more garlic for the beans.

"Is Nona staying here with you?" Abuelita asked Mami. Nona was Mami's younger sister, and she lived in the Dominican Republic. She was coming to visit in a few days.

"No, she's staying in a hotel."

"That's ridiculous! She has family to stay with!"

"I guess she thought everybody would be more comfortable this way." Mami put the garlic cloves in the mortar and sprinkled salt on them.

"She would be comfortable in my house," Abuelita said.

Mami gave Abuelita her version of my are-you-an-idiot look. "You live in a studio apartment with just one bed."

"You and your sisters slept together in one bed your whole childhood. You were comfortable, weren't you?"

Mami smiled and shook her head. "We're not children anymore, Mamá." She pounded the garlic over and over, then looked back up at Abuelita. "Nona says she has a surprise for us."

"Is it presents?" Connie said.

I kept my eyes on the cucumbers. My aunt had told me about her surprise the last time we spoke, but I had promised to keep it a secret.

"Maybe," Mami said. She stood up and stirred the mashed garlic into the beans.

Abuelita clasped her hands together. "Maybe Nona's getting married!" My grandmother always complained about Tía Nona being an "old maid." "Nona's going to stay a *solterona* if she doesn't apply herself," she said about once a week.

"Well, she has been talking about Juan Miguel a lot lately," Mami said.

"He comes from a good family too," Abuelita said. "He should have good intentions."

Mami nodded. "It sounds like he makes Nona very happy. But we don't know if that's her surprise, so let's not get too excited."

Papi walked in the door. "Papi!" Connie and Rosie ran up to him and climbed onto his shoulders.

"I am so hungry." Papi used his Big Bad Giant voice. "These two little girls look delicious!" Connie and Rosie giggled as he pretended to gobble them up.

"Okay, girls," Mami said. "It's time to wash your hands and set the table for dinner. Let's get an extra chair for Abuelita."

"Oh, I'm not staying today," Abuelita said. She stood up, her mouth spreading into a huge smile. "Lalo's taking me out to dinner for my birthday."

"Your birthday?" I said. "That was a month ago." I remembered because Mami had made all of Abuelita's favorites for dinner and we baked her a cake. Mami's brother, Tío Lalo, was invited, but he never showed up.

"Well, he's been very busy."

"Doing what?" I should have known better than to say anything, but it just came out. By the time I noticed Mami and Papi shaking their heads, it was too late.

"He has a new job! And it's hard work lifting all those packages in that warehouse, so he gets very tired. But they love him already, so I'm sure he'll keep this job for a long time!"

"Well, that's wonderful," Papi said. "I wish him the best of luck."

"Are you saying he needs luck? That he's not smart and hardworking and deserving of a good job?"

"Of course not, Mamá," Mami said. "It's just an expression."

"I know you have no faith in your brother," Abuelita said. She turned to Papi. "And neither does your husband. And now"—she pointed at me—"now your obnoxious daughter is attacking her own uncle!" She held her head up and marched to the door. "If you can't respect my son, then I'm not welcome here." She opened the door and out she went, slamming the door behind her.

We all stood there and looked at the closed door.

"I'm sorry," I said. "I didn't mean to upset her. I was just asking a question."

Papi shrugged. "She'll get over it."

Mami nodded. "I'll bring her a plate after we finish eating. She'll probably be hungry by then."

Of course we assumed Tío Lalo wouldn't come through. Again. And Abuelita would be back at our house the next day and she would sit in the dining room, sideways in her chair, her hands folded over her lap, and tell Mami the proper way to fry plantains. She wouldn't even mention her little outburst.

Chapter 4

DURING DINNER WE TALKED ABOUT Tía Nona's visit. "She'll be here in time for your eighth-grade graduation!" Mami said to Gracie.

"Is Tía Nona bringing me a present?" Connie said. "She didn't bring me anything last time."

"You weren't even born yet last time!" Rosie pressed her forehead into her palm.

"I know. So I didn't get a present. It's not fair!"

Mami laughed. "I don't know if she's had a chance to buy any presents. She was in Madrid for only a week, and she was working the whole time. The important thing is that we get to see her again. That's her gift to us."

"What's she like?" Connie asked Gracie.

"Oh, she's beautiful," Gracie said. "She's always smiling, and she has dimples, just like you."

"Really?!"

"Yes, you look a lot like your Tía Nona," Mami said.

Gracie turned to me. "Do you remember her dimples, Anamay?"

"I remember that she's really smart," I said. "She's the only one in Mami's family to go to college."

"That's right," Mami said. "She always had her nose in a book when we were kids, just like Anamay."

"She gave me my first book," I said. "Since Papi hates to buy books."

Papi was piling our plates with salad. He stopped and pointed the tongs at me. "Ana María, if we bought you every book you wanted to read, we'd be broke," he said. Newsflash: We were already broke. "New York City has a wonderful public library system," Papi continued. "There is no reason whatsoever to waste money on so many books."

Papi just didn't get me. But Tía Nona did. Whenever she called Mami, she always spoke with me too. There was so much to tell her about the things I was learning and doing, and she always listened. Plus, she had so many interesting stories to share with me. Her conversations with my sisters were way short. I knew she asked to talk to them just to be polite.

"Tía Nona loves to travel," I said to Connie. "She's been to about twenty different countries, and she speaks four languages. Now she's learning Chinese. She says it's really hard." I sat back and folded my arms across my chest. There was more to say, but Tía Nona's secret was safe with me.

"Are you going to be a doctor like Tía Nona?" Rosie asked me. Her mouth was full of rice.

"I don't know. Maybe," I said. Sick people and blood grossed me out, but I didn't want to say no absolutely. I mean, if Tía Nona liked being a doctor, maybe I could like it too.

"I think Ana María would make a great lawyer," Papi said. "You know she can't lose an argument."

"What do you mean?" I asked. "I never argue with anyone. When have you ever heard me argue with people?"

Papi laughed, and Mami and my sisters joined him. I had to smile too. After all, maybe I did sometimes argue a little, like now.

"It's not an insult, Ana María," Papi said. "I just mean that you're good with words and with proving a point. In fact, you should come to work with me one day. I think you'll really like it."

I knew Papi loved his job helping out clients who lived in awful places and could barely afford food for their kids. But if I ever became a lawyer, I wanted to be the making-a-lot-of-money kind, like Claudia's parents. "Hmm, I don't know, maybe," I said. I put a forkful of codfish in my mouth and concentrated on my plate.

"Maybe you could go to work with Tía Nona, and see if you like that?" Rosie said to me.

Papi chuckled. "Well, that would be a very long commute to the Dominican Republic." He put his fork down and rubbed his chin. "But you know what, Ana María? I have a friend from college who's a physician. I'm sure he would let you tag along with him at work one day."

"Okay, maybe." I was getting queasy just thinking about it.

"What about you, Altagracia? Have you thought about your future?"

Oh, good. Now Papi would remind Gracie—again—that she needed to apply herself in high school if she wanted to go anywhere in life. Gracie would whine that she tried her best and Bs weren't so bad and what did he expect from her. Then Mami would jump in and tell Papi he was being too hard on Gracie. By the end of all that drama, Papi would have forgotten all about me following anybody around at work. I scooped some beans over my rice and sat back to enjoy the show.

"I want to be a fashion designer," Gracie said.

"I don't know any fashion designers, but I'll ask around," Papi said.

"I'm going to be a dancer and a chef and an actress and a teacher." Rosie ticked off each job on a finger.

"Wow! You'll be very busy," Papi said. "But I'm sure you can do it."

"I want to be just like Mami when I grow up!" Connie always figured out how to get an *"Ay, qué linda"*—"Oh, how cute"—from Mami. And lucky Gracie got off easy this time.

* * *

After dinner I washed the dishes and Gracie dried. We were quiet for a while. I thought about Lincoln Center, the scholarship to the Eleanor School, and whether I really had

26

a shot at either one. I'd looked at the scholarship application and it required that I do a bunch of stuff: write two essays, complete a super long questionnaire about my current and career interests, and get three letters of recommendation. That would be a lot of work. And even though I loved playing the piano, just thinking about performing in front of an audience was making my stomach flutter. If I went to the Eleanor School, I could work on my stage fright by joining the debate team or even the theater club. We didn't have either of those at my current school.

"Why do you hate me?" Gracie asked out of the blue.

"What are you talking about?"

"Why don't you want me to make your dress? You know I can do a good job."

"Actually, I don't know that," I said. "And I don't hate you. I just want to wear something normal. I don't want to stand out and have everyone say 'Look at the girl with the homemade dress.'"

"I promise you it'll be normal, and really nice. You know Mami will make sure it's perfect."

She had a point. "It doesn't matter, anyway. I'm probably not going to Lincoln Center."

"Why? Were you nervous? Did you make mistakes? It's that Doña Dulce. Nobody can play well with those beady eyes staring at you."

"No, it's not that. I just think the association people didn't like me."

"Why wouldn't they like you?"

She was kidding, right? Even my own grandmother said I was obnoxious. "I corrected one of them when he called me Ann Marie."

"Oh." Gracie plucked a plate out of the drying rack with a clink.

I poured soap onto the sponge and squished it against a greasy bowl. The warm water hissed as it snaked its way across the dirty dishes and down the drain. "Would you have done that if it were you?" I asked.

Gracie thought about it. "I don't know. I mean, 'Ana María' shouldn't be that hard for people to say, so I can see why you expect everyone to get it right. I never bother when someone gets my name wrong because—let's face it—'Altagracia' is pretty weird. I don't know what Mami and Papi were thinking when they picked it."

"They were thinking that Altagracia is the patron saint of the DR," I said. "They were thinking that you're special." Unlike boring me with my simple name.

"Yeah, I guess. But, anyway, I'm sure those music people just want good piano players, and you're fabulous. They probably forgot about the name incident as soon as you walked out the door."

"I hope so."

"I'll keep my fingers crossed," Gracie said. "And if you don't want me to make your dress, I'll just tell Mami I don't think I can handle it, okay?"

"Okay. Thanks." We continued with the dishes in silence. I thought about how happy I feel when I play the piano well. Then I thought about Gracie and how much she loved to sew. I had to admit she was pretty good at it. "Gracie?"

"Yeah?"

"I want you to make my dress. With Mami's help, of course."

Gracie squealed. Her eyes shone and her mouth hung open. "Are you sure?"

I nodded.

"Okay, well, I have some great ideas. It should be sparkly, but not too much, and long, of course, and probably satin, or maybe lace . . ." She kept describing this dress as she threw her arms around me. She was way too huggy.

Chapter 5

I WAS PRACTICING PIANO THE NEXT DAY when the intercom buzzed. "I wonder who that is," Mami said. "We aren't expecting anyone." Mami shouldn't have been surprised. People always showed up without even calling. She put down the laundry she was folding and pressed the intercom button. "Who is it?" she shouted into the speaker.

"It's Chichi," a voice crackled. Ugh. Mami's so-called friend. She was probably bringing her two brats over for Mami to babysit, *again*. Mami buzzed her in.

My sisters burst out of our room. "Are Jennie and Lisa with her?" Rosie asked.

"I don't know, *mija*," Mami said. "We'll see when she gets here."

"I want to show them my new Barbie," Connie said.

Poor Connie really thought a hand-me-down doll became new just because Mami made a new outfit for it. And why did she like to play with Jennie and Lisa anyway? They were just a couple of five-year-old bullies. I couldn't stand how mean they were to Connie. She always forgot about their constant teasing, until they made her cry. Then I would have to scoop her up, find a quiet spot, and cuddle her until she calmed down. It happened every time.

I slipped down the hall into my room and closed the door. I took out one of the math worksheets Mr. Briller gave me to study for the Eleanor scholarship exam. Why couldn't everything in life be like math? You pay attention, maybe study a little, and then you get it. After that, there isn't a single problem you can't solve. Every answer you come up with is either right or wrong. And there's only one right answer. No discussion. No disagreement.

"What a pleasant surprise!" I could hear Mami's smiling voice through our thin walls.

"I hope this isn't a bad time," Chichi said.

"Oh, no, no, no," Mami said.

"Where are they? Where are they?" I could picture Connie running around looking for Jennie and Lisa, as if they could be hiding in the folds of Chichi's skirt.

"My girls are home with Lydia," Chichi said. "This is just a quick visit. Gracie's dress came in today, but the stores were so busy that we didn't get a chance to call you. I'm on my way home, so I brought it over."

Two weeks earlier, we had gone to Chichi's Children's Clothing to buy a dress for Gracie's graduation. Chichi didn't have anything that fit Gracie, but her sister's store, Lydia's

Ladies' Fashions, was right next door. Gracie found something there she liked, but the color she wanted was out, so Lydia ordered it for her.

"Ohhh," I heard Gracie say. "It's gorgeous! I'm going to try it on right now." She burst into our room, holding up a teal dress with a pleated skirt that fell just below her knees. "Isn't it perfect?"

I shrugged.

She closed the door and started taking off her clothes. "I sure hope this looks good," she said. "Graduation is only two days away. Where will I find another dress at this late date?" She slipped into the dress. "Anamay, can you zip this up for me?"

I blew out loudly through my mouth and tossed my worksheet aside. As I pulled the zipper up, I noticed that the dress really *was* pretty, and so soft. And teal was a perfect color for Gracie. She twirled around and her long hair swirled in rhythm with her skirt.

"Oh, it's so beautiful!" she exclaimed.

Gracie seemed so happy. Why wouldn't she be happy? Everyone was making a big deal out of this dumb graduation of hers, like nobody had ever finished eighth grade before. Papi was even taking the day off of work for it.

Papi didn't go to my elementary school graduation the year before. Not even after the principal called to tell him he might want to be there. "I didn't go to Altagracia's," Papi had said, "so it wouldn't be right." Abuelita had stayed home to babysit Connie and Rosie so they wouldn't disrupt the ceremony, and Gracie had a final exam, so she couldn't come either. So Mami was the only person from my family clapping every time the principal called my name.

Not to brag, but he called my name a lot. Gold Medal for Outstanding Achievement in Math: Ana María Reyes. The Silver Medal went to my friend, Ruben Rivera. Gold Medal for Outstanding Achievement in Science: Ana María Reyes. Again, Ruben got the silver. Everyone clapped at first. Some of the other kids even cheered. Gold Medal for Outstanding Achievement in Reading: Ana María Reyes. In Writing: Ana María Reyes. I thought I heard some groans. In Physical Education: some other kid. Clapping and cheering. Ruben got the gold for social studies, but I got the silver. Light, polite applause. People were mumbling about how sick they were of hearing our two names over and over. Finally, Mami and I walked out of there with my six gold and three silver medals.

"Oh, Anamay, I'm so proud of you!" Mami gave me a big hug. "But maybe you should put those awards away when we get home," she said. "Your sister might feel badly if she sees them." Because Gracie of the skin with no pimples, the never-needed-braces teeth, and the 20/20 vision could never know that she was less than perfect. Now here she was, swinging around in her teal dress and thinking she was just so special because she was accomplishing a goal most people in prison have already met.

"Well?" She looked at me and raised her eyebrows. "Aren't you excited for me?"

"Yeah, whatever," I said.

Gracie ran out of the room to model for the crowd in the living room. "Oh, how beautiful!" Mami said.

"It's a perfect fit," Chichi said.

"Sooo pretty," Rosie and Connie said at the same time.

How annoying. But so what if my parents cared more about Gracie's feelings than mine? So what if we had one more kid to clutter up this family? I would keep reading, studying, and practicing piano. I would get a full scholarship to the Eleanor School and get a fabulous education there. Yes, I could have a great life in spite of my family. I went back to multiplying and dividing decimal numbers. I definitely got every answer right.

Chapter 6

WHEN MAMI OPENED THE DOOR FOR Tía Nona on Thursday afternoon, my aunt was holding hands with a tall, skinny man. She let go of him and hurled herself onto Mami. They hugged and laughed and cried. Finally, they pulled away from each other but kept their hands locked together.

"This is my sister, Mecho," Tía Nona said to the man. "Mecho, this is Juan Miguel."

Juan Miguel was wearing white shoes, white pants, and a pale green shirt that matched Tía Nona's dress. He and Mami hugged like they were old friends who hadn't seen each other in a long time. "I've heard so much about you!" Mami said. "Welcome, welcome!" She pulled him into the living room. "These are my girls." She introduced us one at a time, and we all hugged him too, but not like old friends.

"So this is the famous Anamay?" Juan Miguel said when he got to me. "I've heard a lot about you."

"You should hear Anamay play the piano," Tía Nona said. "She was already marvelous five years ago when she had only been playing for a little while, so I can just imagine how much better she is now!"

"Yes, each of my girls has her own special talent," Mami said.

I frowned at my mother. She always had to bring my sisters into everything.

"Mecho's expecting again," Tía Nona said to Juan Miguel.

"Congratulations! You have a beautiful family."

Mami smiled. "Thank you."

"Maybe this time you'll have an *hombrecito* to take care of his sisters," Juan Miguel said.

"That's our hope," Mami said.

Oh brother.

"Is this Consuelito?" Tía Nona got down on one knee, held Connie's hands, and looked straight into her face. "You're right, Mecho, she does look like me!"

Connie loved that. She pointed at Juan Miguel. "Is he your boyfriend?"

Tía Nona and Juan Miguel laughed. "Yes," Tía Nona said.

"Are you getting married?"

More laughter, but there wasn't an answer this time. Of course, I already knew the answer, but I wondered when they planned to tell the rest of the family. "You're such a big girl!" Tía Nona said. "I imagined you as a little baby. How old are you now?"

Connie held up three fingers.

"My goodness, you're almost all grown up!"

"And I'm very mature for my age," Connie said.

There was a knock at the door. Abuelita burst in with a scream and threw herself at Tía Nona, who screamed back. The two of them held on to each other for a long time. When they finally let go, Abuelita's cheeks were wet and her eye makeup was a little smudged. Then she noticed Juan Miguel. "And who is this handsome young man?" she said.

"Mamá, this is Juan Miguel."

Abuelita reached up to wrap her arms around Juan Miguel's neck. Another long-lost-old-friend hug.

"Where's Tavito?" Tía Nona asked.

Mami looked at the clock on the wall. "He should be home from work soon."

"What about Lalo? Is he coming?"

"Well, I invited him," Mami said.

"Oh, he'll be here," Abuelita said. "Unless he gets tied up at work. He has a new job, you know."

"Well, while we wait, I'll give the girls a few little presents I got for them in Spain." Tía Nona reached into the brown tote bag that hung from her shoulder.

Connie jumped up and down. "Presents, presents, presents!"

Tía Nona laughed. "All right, calm down." She handed each of us a little wooden box. We pried them open right away.

"Oh, castanets," Rosie said. "We learned about these

37

in dance class!" She lifted her castanets out of the box and looped them onto her thumbs. The rest of us copied her and started clacking away.

"And one more thing," Tía Nona said. She took out a giant book and handed it to me. "*Don Quixote*. It's a classic."

"Thanks, Tía Nona!" I hugged my aunt, and then opened the book. I flipped through a few pages and glanced at the long Spanish words. Reading this book was going to be a fun challenge.

Rosie peeked inside Tía Nona's bag. "Do I get a book too?"

"Oh, I'm sorry, no," Tía Nona said. "I know how much Anamay likes to read, so I picked that up for her. But you like your castanets, right?"

"Of course she does," Mami said. "Thank you so much, Nona. But you really shouldn't have gone to the trouble to get an extra gift for Anamay."

I couldn't believe Mami said that. Why didn't she want me to have anything special? But before Tía Nona could answer, Papi walked in the door. The introductions and hugs started all over again.

When everyone was settled in the living room, Tía Nona said, "Juan Miguel and I have an important announcement."

"But Lalo isn't here yet," Abuelita said.

Tía Nona looked at Mami and raised her eyebrows just a little.

"Should we eat dinner first, while we wait for him?" Mami asked.

"And eat without him? That would be rude," Abuelita answered.

"Mamá, we can't sit here all night waiting for Lalo," Mami said. "The girls will have to get ready for bed in a few hours."

Abuelita sat up and breathed out hard. "Well, okay. Let's hear your news, Nona."

Tía Nona looked at me and winked. I smiled and nodded so she would know I hadn't given anything away.

Juan Miguel stood up and cleared his throat. "Señora Castillo, Mecho, Tavito, *muchachas*, I love Nona very much, and it would be an honor to join your wonderful family and spend the rest of my life with her. Therefore"—he turned to Abuelita and took a deep breath—"I ask your permission and your blessing to marry your daughter."

"*Ay, gracias a Dios!*" Abuelita looked at the ceiling in thanks to God. Then she jumped up and hugged Juan Miguel and Tía Nona. Soon she was crying again.

"The wedding will be in August," Tía Nona said. "That way all of you can come without missing any school."

I looked at my parents and waited. Ever since Tía Nona told me about her engagement last week, I had wondered about this moment. I had never been to the Dominican Republic nor met more than half of my family, and I was excited about the trip. But my parents were sure to say we couldn't afford the six airplane tickets. Maybe Mami would go alone. Or she would bring Gracie because she's the oldest, or Connie because she's the youngest. Or even Rosie for some reason. But I was the one that belonged at Tía Nona's wedding. Everyone should know that.

Mami cried and hugged Tía Nona. "This is so exciting! My baby sister getting married! I wouldn't miss it for the world."

Papi cleared his throat. "Of course Mecho will be there," he said. "We would all love to go, but I don't know if that's possible."

"Oh, Tavito, all of you have to come! Juan Miguel and I will pay for everything."

"Yes, absolutely," Juan Miguel said. "Money is not a problem."

"That's very generous, but I can't accept."

"But I need the whole family at my wedding!" Tía Nona started to cry.

"Let's not talk about this right now," Mami said. "It's time for dinner. Don't worry, Nona, we'll figure out a way." She put her arm around Tía Nona and led her into the kitchen.

As promised, nobody talked about our going to the wedding during dinner. Abuelita grilled Juan Miguel about his family and his work. He smiled as he answered all her questions, but Tía Nona scowled. "Mamá, you already know all about Juan Miguel and his family. I told you everything about him when you asked me all those same questions."

"Well, I'm an old lady, I can't remember so many details."

Tía Nona rolled her eyes, and Mami came to the rescue. "Are you going someplace fun for your honeymoon?"

Tía Nona put her fork down and rested her chin on top of her interlaced fingers. Her dimples were super deep now. "Juan Miguel is being very mysterious about the honeymoon. I've been instructed to take two weeks off of work, and to pack swimwear and evening dresses. But he won't tell me anything else."

Juan Miguel put his thumb and forefinger together, twisted his hand in front of his mouth, then tossed an imaginary thing to the side. "My lips are locked," he said, "and I have thrown away the key." His white teeth sparkled.

"Aw, that's so romantic." Mami smiled and looked at Papi. Mami thinks everything is romantic. For their honeymoon, she and Papi took the ferry to the Statue of Liberty with a picnic lunch. They snapped lots of pictures when they reached the top of the statue and then they went back to Manhattan for dinner in Chinatown. Mami says it was a clear day and the view of the city from the ferry was beautiful.

Papi was staring down at his food, and did not look up.

"Have you picked out your dress yet?" Abuelita asked Tía Nona.

"Yes, let me show you." Tía Nona got up and went into the living room to reach into her bag. She came back and handed a photo to Abuelita.

Abuelita squinted at the picture as she held it with her arm stretched out in front of her. "Oh," she said with a frown. "You're going to wear this to a church?"

Tía Nona closed her eyes and took a few deep breaths. "What's wrong with the dress, Mamá?"

"Well, it's so . . . revealing. It doesn't seem appropriate for a decent woman."

My aunt rolled her eyes again and looked at Mami.

"May I see it?" Gracie asked. "Oh, it's beautiful," she said as she looked at the photo. "Strapless dresses are really in style!"

Abuelita opened her mouth but Mami came to the rescue again. "So, tomorrow is our Altagracia's big day!"

Tía Nona nodded. "We're so excited about it! Should we come here, or meet you at the school?"

Then Mami went on and on about the details of Gracie's graduation, where to meet, what time, blah, blah, blah. We never got back to talking about the wedding. Actually, Papi didn't say a word the whole dinner. I couldn't believe I had the chance to visit another country, meet the rest of my family, and go to my favorite aunt's wedding, and Papi might ruin it by being so stubborn. Maybe there was a way to convince him to let us go. There had to be. I would come up with some good reasons and talk him into it. But I had to do it fast.

Chapter 7

T HE NEXT DAY, THE SCHOOL GYM was filled with folding chairs facing the stage, all ready for graduation. Mami and Papi got there early and saved eight seats together for our whole family. A very pregnant woman rushed in when the ceremony was just starting and paced up and down the aisles, looking for an empty seat. Mami waved her over, then put Connie on her lap so the woman could sit in Connie's seat. Abuelita got all bent out of shape about that. "Now where's Lalo going to sit?" she said in a much-too-loud whisper. Mami didn't answer.

First Sarita Gómez played "The Star-Spangled Banner" on the piano. I listened closely as she played. Doña Dulce said I had perfected the national anthem when she taught me to play it last year. But Sarita's version seemed kind of different. Better. Maybe it was all that extra time she got to practice alone in Doña Dulce's house. Everyone clapped and cheered when Sarita finished. Some people had tears in their eyes.

Everything after that was super boring. The principal gave a long speech about impressive young men and women making their families and community proud. Then he handed out the awards. Sarita got one for music. A whole bunch of kids got awards for making honor roll every year, meaning they never got anything worse than a B. When they called Gracie's name, Mami nudged Papi with her elbow and said, "You see, she's a good student." Papi picked up the camera and snapped a picture of Gracie holding her certificate and shaking hands with the principal. It was a good thing he got that photo, because Gracie didn't get any more awards.

Gracie ran up to us after the ceremony and started the hugs. Tía Nona and Juan Miguel told her she looked beautiful in her teal dress, and Abuelita grabbed Gracie's face and planted a big red kiss on her forehead. Papi said he was very proud and that he had taken a great photo of her.

Then we heard a voice shout, "Hello, hello, hello!" It was Tío Lalo walking toward us with a ginormous bouquet of roses.

Papi leaned down and muttered in Mami's ear, "I hope he didn't steal those."

Thank goodness Abuelita didn't hear that. She would have flipped out.

"Where is the beautiful graduate?" Tío Lalo gave the flowers to Gracie and hugged her tightly. "Now, let's celebrate!" he shouted. He raised his arms in the air and stumbled a little. Some of the other students and their families glanced at my uncle, then turned away quickly.

"Lalo, *mi amor*, keep your voice down." Abuelita put a hand on Tío Lalo's arm. "Now, let me introduce you. Juan Miguel, this is my only son, Lalo. Since my late husband is no longer with us, God rest his soul, Lalo will walk Nona down the aisle at the wedding."

Tío Lalo and Tía Nona both seemed shocked at this news, but Tío Lalo recovered quickly. "My baby sister is getting married? Oh my goodness!" He grabbed Tía Nona and kissed her hard on the cheek, then shook Juan Miguel's hand and slapped his back. "We should celebrate with a drink."

"Surprise, surprise," Papi mumbled. My uncle always said he liked to have a little drink "every now and then." According to Papi, that meant *every* now and *every* then.

"Hi, Anamay." I turned around. It was Sarita with the pregnant woman. "This is my sister, Lucy." Lucy didn't look much older than Sarita.

"Hi," I said. "Um, congratulations, Sarita."

"Thanks!" she said. Then we just stood there and looked at each other. I realized I had never had a conversation with Sarita before, and I didn't know what else to say.

Mami stepped in. "Hello, Sarita! I met you a few years ago at Doña Dulce's. How you've grown since then! And you played beautifully today. It was the best part of the graduation."

"Definitely!" I said, nodding my head.

Sarita looked down at her shoes and smiled just a little bit. "Thank you."

"Do you play the piano too?" Mami asked Lucy.

"Oh, no, that's Sarita's thing. I'm still trying to figure out what I'm good at." Lucy put one hand on top of her belly and one underneath. "Maybe I'll be a good mom."

"I'm sure you will be," Mami said. "Is your family doing anything to celebrate today?" she asked Sarita.

"No, my father's working and . . ." Sarita bit her lower lip. "We don't really have a mom anymore."

Oh no. Mami would want to adopt them now.

"Then you should come over and celebrate with us!" she said.

I knew it.

"No, I couldn't," Sarita said. "It's Gracie's party."

"Gracie won't mind at all."

"What won't I mind at all?" Gracie had wandered off to chat with her friends, but now she was right next to us, her arms full of roses. Papi always joked that the best way to get Gracie's attention was to whisper her name from three blocks away.

"I've invited Sarita and her sister to your graduation party," Mami said.

"Oh, good! It'll be so much fun!"

Sarita smiled for real this time. "Okay. Thanks."

Mami fished a piece of paper out of her purse and wrote

down our address. Sarita studied the note. "Is that the tall brick building at the top of the hill?" she asked.

Mami nodded.

"Wow. That's a nice building."

"It's the Reyes castle!" Mami laughed as she said that.

"Can our two little brothers come?" Lucy said. "We need to pick them up from school soon."

"From the elementary school?" Mami said.

Lucy and Sarita nodded.

"They had a half day today," Mami said. "Your brothers got out at eleven thirty."

"Oh." Lucy looked at Sarita and shrugged. "I guess we should go now."

Wow, I thought. Rosie would freak out if she ever got picked up from school four hours late.

"Well, go, go, go!" Mami said. "We'll meet the four of you back at our house."

"Mami, can Pedro come too?" Gracie asked. Pedro walked home with us from school every day, even though he lived in the opposite direction. He looked different now, staring at the floor as he stood behind Gracie, all dressed up with his hair parted to the side and greased down.

"Who's Pedro?" Papi said. Gracie introduced them, and Papi shook Pedro's hand and asked to meet his family.

"My parents had to work," Pedro said. "It's just me here today."

"Of course you can come to our house." Mami touched Pedro's arm and smiled, and it looked like she wanted to adopt him too. How many kids did she want anyway?

Chapter 8

WHEN MAMI PLANNED GRACIE'S GRADUATION PARTY, it was supposed to be a quiet family gathering. But with Pedro, Sarita and her family, and a couple more friends whose parents weren't around to celebrate with them, it was way hectic. Sarita's brothers were like the wild dog pups I saw on a field trip to the Bronx Zoo. The boys jumped on each other for no reason, rolled around on the ground wrestling, and almost knocked Abuelita down twice. Pedro kept telling jokes and making Gracie and her friends, Vicky and Rebecca, laugh and laugh. Once Vicky spat out a whole meatball, and Rebecca had lemonade coming out of her nose. Gross. But no one was as bad as Tío Lalo in party mode. "Anamay, play something on the piano so I can sing along," he said, swinging around a beer. Then he started singing—badly—some weird old-timey Spanish song from his childhood. I did not want to be a part of that, so I threw Sarita under the bus.

"She'll play for you," I said to Tío Lalo. "She's much better than me anyway." Which was true. But Sarita didn't seem fazed. She sat down at the piano and looked at my uncle expectantly.

"Play the merengue that has the trombone part," Tío Lalo said. Guess how many merengues have trombone parts? All of them. But still, Sarita didn't squint at my uncle and say "Huh?" like I would have done. She just nodded, put her hands on the keys, and trilled out some beautiful notes. Tío Lalo smiled, closed his eyes, and started to serenade an imaginary dance partner. Soon everyone was clapping and singing along. Abuelita and Juan Miguel scooted the coffee table aside to make a dance floor. Even my parents danced, Papi with Connie standing on his shoes, and Mami with Rosie twirling around and around.

My family never had this much fun when I played the piano.

After the party, Papi and I walked Sarita and her family home. Sarita and I followed behind her brothers, who were taking turns giving each other piggyback rides. Papi and Lucy were in front of the boys. I heard him say "GED test" and "cost-free babysitting" and "happy to help you." I smiled. Classic Papi.

"Do you know if you're going to Lincoln Center?" Sarita asked me.

"No. Hasn't Doña Dulce told you yet?"

Sarita shook her head.

"Well, of course you're going. It's the second person I wonder about," I said.

"What are you talking about?" Sarita said. "I don't know if I'm going."

"Oh, come on, you're Doña Dulce's favorite."

"No, I'm not," Sarita said. "Plus I don't even think it's her decision."

"But you are really good," I said. "You're definitely the best of Doña Dulce's students." I hated to admit that, but I knew it was true.

"Oh, Anamay, you are so sweet to say that! But you're really good too."

No one had ever called me sweet before. I bit back a smile. "So, what will you play if you go?" I asked.

"Hmm, I don't know. I'd probably talk it over with Doña Dulce. There are so many beautiful pieces to choose from."

"What about that Chopin piece I've heard you play?" I said. "Polonaise in G Minor. I can't believe how well you play that. I've tried it, and I just can't get the hang of it."

Sarita looked at me and smiled. "Hmm, maybe. What about you? What would you play?"

I stepped over a rut in the sidewalk and concentrated on avoiding the cracks. "I wish I could play something other than classical music," I said. "I taught myself to play some Alicia Keys songs, and my friend Claudia sings along. She's got a great voice, and it's more fun to play songs that have lyrics. They make more sense."

"More sense? How?"

"Well, that way I know if a song is happy, sad, or what."

"Oh, that's interesting," Sarita said. "I never thought of that. Usually, the notes, melody, and tempo speak to me. Words aren't necessary."

Maybe that explained why Sarita was so good. I wondered if I could learn to understand music like that.

Papi held the door open for us when we got to Sarita's building. The boys tumbled toward the stairs. "Wait," Papi said. He pressed the elevator button.

"Oh, that doesn't work," Lucy said. She held on to the banister and climbed up behind her brothers. Papi followed them. Sarita and I were still at the back.

As we passed by Doña Dulce's apartment on the second floor, Sarita said, "Should we ask about Lincoln Center?"

I looked at her. Would Doña Dulce be annoyed? Probably. I shook my head. We kept going.

By the time we got to the sixth floor, I was breathing loudly. Papi took a handkerchief out of his pocket and dabbed the sweat off his forehead. Sarita and her family weren't even a little out of breath.

Lucy took out her key, then turned to her brothers and whispered, "Remember, Papi's asleep, so be quiet." She unlocked the door and they stormed inside. "Would you like to come in and have a glass of lemonade?" Lucy asked Papi and me.

My mouth watered.

"No, thank you, we have to go now," Papi said. Papi never wanted to be "an imposition."

"Thank you for inviting us to your wonderful party, Mr. Reyes," Sarita said. "Papi's going to love this food." She pointed with her chin at the foil-covered plate in her hands.

"He sure is," Lucy said. "Your wife's cooking is way better than mine, and Papi's always starving before his night job."

"It was our pleasure," Papi said. "And remember to call us if you need anything."

As Papi and I walked downstairs, I thought about how I would have him all to myself for the whole walk home, and I knew just what to talk about. I had come up with all my arguments last night before bed. When we got outside, I said, "Why don't you want us to go to the DR?"

"It's not that, Ana María. I would love it if we could all go, but we just can't afford it." Papi put his hands in his pockets and walked with long strides.

I ran to keep up. "But Tía Nona and Juan Miguel said they'd pay for it."

"It wouldn't be right to make them pay for us."

"Why not? You heard Juan Miguel. His family has a ton of money. His parents own all those hotels, and he had a nanny when he was a kid!"

Papi chuckled. "Just because they have more money than we do doesn't mean they should pay for our trips."

I had expected him to say that, and I was ready to make my case. "First of all, you're always giving people money just because they have less than we do. I've seen you do it lots of times. If that's okay, then this should be too."

Papi lifted his eyebrows and nodded slightly, but he didn't say anything.

"Second of all, you and Mami always say that family connections are important, but we kids don't even know half our family. We've never met your brothers and their kids, or Mami's other sister and her family. This would be our chance to get to know them."

Papi looked at me and smiled. I decided to close with my best argument of all.

"And finally, they're not paying for a fancy vacation for us. It's so Tía Nona can have the wedding she always wanted—one with her whole family there. Would you tell her she can't wear the wedding dress of her dreams just because you can't afford to buy it? Of course not!"

Papi stopped walking and looked at me. "You know what, Ana María? You really should be a lawyer. Those are excellent points. And, like I said before, you never lose an argument." He pulled me close and kissed the top of my head. Then we started to walk again, his hand resting on my shoulder.

I had convinced him. I could tell. And maybe he was right about this lawyer thing. We didn't say anything more the rest of the way home, but Papi whistled one of the tunes Sarita had played at the party, and I couldn't stop smiling.

Chapter 9

PAPI CALLED ANOTHER FAMILY MEETING WHEN we got home from Sarita's house. "Ana María and I spoke, and she made some compelling arguments," he said. "So I have decided—if your mother agrees—that it would be appropriate to allow Nona to pay for our trip to her wedding."

My sisters and I jumped and cheered, and Mami put her arms around Papi. This was way better than our last family meeting.

Tía Nona rushed over the next morning as soon as Mami told her we would go to the wedding. She drew me into a hug and whispered in my ear, "I'm not surprised it was you who convinced your father. Thank you, my smart girl."

I breathed in the familiar smell of baby powder from her neck. "You're welcome," I whispered back.

Tía Nona kept one arm around my shoulders and turned to the rest of my family. "Let's buy these plane tickets!"

"I already found some flights that work for us," Papi said from the computer desk.

Tía Nona walked across the room and leaned over Papi's shoulder. Her eyes moved back and forth across the screen. "Don't you want to fly first class?" she said.

"No, that's not necessary."

"But —"

"These flights are perfect," Mami said. She put one arm around Tía Nona and one hand on Papi's shoulder.

Tía Nona reached in her bag and pulled out a credit card.

After Papi punched in the numbers of my aunt's card, I let go of the breath I had been holding in. I heard Gracie do the same thing next to me.

"Now that that's taken care of," Tía Nona said, "we need to get the girls dresses to wear to the wedding." She looked at Mami and asked, "Do you have time to go shopping today?"

"Nona, you don't have to do that," Papi said. "We'll make sure they wear something nice."

"But I want all my nieces to match, and I promised Muñeca a dress from New York, so it's only fair that I buy dresses for your girls too!" Muñeca was the daughter of Mami's older sister, Tía Chea. Mami and Tía Chea wrote letters to each other, and sometimes my aunt sent us pictures of her family, but we had never met them.

Papi opened his mouth like he was about to say something, then he stopped and looked at Mami. She tilted her head a little and gave him begging eyes. Papi closed his mouth tight and sat on the couch. When we walked out the door, he was engrossed in the *New York Times*. He only grunted in response to Mami's "We'll see you later, Tavito."

✳ ✳ ✳

"Mecho, why don't you have a car?" Tía Nona asked when we were standing on the subway platform waiting for the train.

"Oh, you don't want to go anywhere in New York City in a car," Mami said. "We'd sit in traffic for hours, then spend the rest of the day looking for a parking spot."

"Well, we could hire someone to drive us," Tía Nona said.

"Ha!" The laugh burst out of Mami, but Tía Nona didn't look amused. Mami reined in her smile and said, "That would be very expensive, Nona. And public transportation works just fine for us."

For her, maybe, I thought. I'd be pretty happy in a comfy car.

The train was crowded but not packed. Mami found three seats together and pulled Rosie and Connie into two of them. "Nona, sit here," she said, pointing to the third seat.

"No, you sit. You're the one that's pregnant."

"Oh, I'm fine. You're not used to riding these trains, so you should sit."

"Mecho, please! I can handle standing in a train. Now, sit."

"No, really, I'm fine."

A teenager with headphones in his ears slipped in front of them and sat in the seat. Mami looked at Tía Nona and shrugged. Tía Nona glared at the boy. "Savages!" she said. He didn't even notice.

We had to switch trains in Times Square. Mami walked behind us with her arms open, trying to keep us all together. She was like one of those triangle things that gathers up balls on a pool table. Tía Nona stopped to watch dancers, musicians, and magicians performing in the station. "Come on, Nona, we need to keep moving," Mami said a few times.

The second train ride wasn't as long as the first one. Pretty soon we were above ground again and walking into Bloomingdale's department store, where Tía Nona had suggested that we go.

"I've never been here before!" Rosie said, looking all around.

"Neither have I," Mami said.

We headed straight to the girls' department. "Let's start with the little ones," Mami said. "Before they get restless."

Mami, Gracie, and Tía Nona looked at every single dress in Connie's and Rosie's sizes. They plucked each one off the rack and had long discussions about their pros and cons.

"This one's too frilly."

"This one's too casual."

"They're going to be hot and sweaty in this one. Remember, August is sweltering in the DR."

"Look at the price of this one!" That was Mami. "And see here!" She held the dress toward Gracie. "It's not even on-grain. Every well-made dress should be on-grain."

It was kind of nice to be in this fancy store and not worry about whether we could afford to buy whatever we wanted. But I wished we could just grab some dresses, pay for them, and go. They all looked equally nice to me, so why did we have to examine each one and talk about it forever and ever? I thought I would die of boredom. Still, I knew Tía Nona wanted her wedding to be perfect, so I tried to help. I wrangled Connie into the dressing room and helped her try on a bunch of dresses. Just when I thought I couldn't take it anymore, Mami and Tía Nona settled on matching yellow cotton dresses for both girls, covered in eyelets arranged in a flower pattern.

"Let's hope we find something similar in the junior section," Tía Nona said.

Connie was super fidgety while Gracie and I tried on dresses. She even got yelled at by some rude saleslady. Fortunately, Tía Nona was there to put that woman in her place. And thank goodness Gracie and I found the perfect yellow dresses to match Connie's and Rosie's. Even though this shopping trip was longer than I thought it needed to be, it was definitely better than shopping with Mami at Chichi's and Lydia's. No looking through sales racks or asking for discounts, or anything else embarrassing like that. Tía Nona didn't gasp or lift her eyebrows when the cashier rang her up. She just smiled and handed the lady her credit card. I was proud to stand next to her, a smile on my face too.

Chapter 10

WE BURST BACK INTO THE APARTMENT like a blustery fall day. Papi was sitting at the dining room table with his checkbook in his hand and a slew of bills spread out in piles. Connie hopped over to him and shoved her new dress in his face. "Isn't it beautiful?" she said.

Papi's lips curved up but his eyes stayed on the papers in front of him. "Yes, beautiful," he said. He started to write a check.

"You didn't even look!" There was no fooling Connie.

"Mine is the same, see?" Rosie waved her dress around. "Gracie and Anamay have yellow dresses too. And we got one more for our cousin in the DR. We'll all match for the wedding!"

Papi nodded. "That's nice." He looked at Mami. "What are we having for dinner?"

"Mecho's tired," Tía Nona said. "Let's get takeout. How about pizza?"

That sounded like a great idea to me. But I knew Mami wouldn't go for it. She thinks the only food that's real is whatever she ate when she was a kid. If a meal doesn't involve rice, beans, or plantains, it's just a snack to her. So she never let us get takeout.

"Pizza, pizza, pizza!" Connie and Rosie jumped up and down, waving their dresses in the air.

Mami looked at Tía Nona and frowned. "Pizza isn't very nutritious," she said. "I can whip something up quickly."

"Oh, Mecho, lighten up," Tía Nona said. "It's just one meal, and you said you're exhausted."

"You do look tired," Papi said. He stood up and cupped Mami's elbow in his hand. "Are your ankles swollen again? Here, sit down." He led her to the sofa. "Rosalba and I will make a salad to have on the side, okay? Pizza's not so bad. Cheese has protein."

Mami let Papi help her onto the couch. "I guess that's okay," she said. "But let's invite Mamá. I know she wants to spend more time with Nona."

"We'll go get her!" Gracie said right away. "Come on, Anamay."

"Why don't we just call her?" I said.

"This way is more personal," Gracie said. "You know how sensitive Abuelita can be. She'll love an in-person invitation." She grabbed my arm and dragged me out before anyone could stop us.

"What is your problem?" I said when we were out in

the hallway. "Why are you being so weird? Well, weirder than usual."

"I just had to get away from Tía Nona," Gracie said. "She's driving me crazy!"

"Why?"

"She's so bossy! I don't know how Mami can stand it." Gracie pressed the down button for the elevator.

"She's not bossy. She just doesn't let people push her around."

"Are you kidding me?" Gracie said. "She was so rude to that poor saleslady, I just wanted to die."

The elevator door opened. "Who? The lady that was mean to Connie?" I said as we stepped inside.

"She was not mean." Gracie pushed the button for the fourth floor. "She just told Connie to stop running around the store."

"Well, Connie's little and she was bored and Mami didn't even stick up for her! She just apologized like a wimp."

"Mami apologized like a polite person," she said. "I can't believe Tía Nona asked to see the manager. That was crazy."

Now we were on four. We stepped out and headed down the narrow hallway. "Well," I said, "like Tía Nona told them, the customer is always right, and she spent a lot of money there, so she's a really good customer."

"You can't be serious!" Gracie said. "Tía Nona's a snob and a bully, and I can't wait for her to leave."

I could not believe my sister. I mean, Tía Nona had just bought us these beautiful dresses, and she was giving us a trip to the Dominican Republic, and this was how Gracie thanked her?

"But you know what?" Gracie said. She stopped suddenly and faced me. "I should have known you would stick up for her. You're a snob too."

"What?!" My voice went up super high. "How am I a snob?"

"Just think about it." Gracie crossed her arms over her chest. "Your best friend in the whole world is a rich girl from Riverdale."

"I thought you liked Claudia!"

"I do like Claudia. But that's not the point. The point is that you think the people in Washington Heights aren't good enough for you."

I looked at Gracie. I had friends in our neighborhood. There was Ruben and . . . well, there was Ruben. But that had nothing to do with the neighborhood. I just didn't make friends as easily as Gracie did. "That's not true," I said. "You don't know what you're talking about."

"Humph." Gracie turned and started walking again.

We stopped in front of Abuelita's apartment. The purple door was still kind of a shocking sight. The building manager told my grandmother she had to paint it dark brown again like all the other doors, and she had smiled and said she would. That was two years ago. Gracie knocked loudly.

Tío Lalo opened Abuelita's door. "Mamá," he called back into the apartment. "It's my two favorite nieces." He always said that, no matter which two nieces were around.

"I didn't know my favorite uncle would be here," Gracie said. She and Tío Lalo laughed and hugged. He reached over with his other arm and pulled me into the group hug. He smelled like beer.

Abuelita and Tío Lalo said yes right away to our pizza-dinner invitation. "But pizza?" Abuelita said. "I'm surprised Mecho's not making something healthier. She's always so picky about food. What's gotten into her?"

"Tía Nona talked her into it," Gracie said.

"And Papi too," I added. Why was she blaming everything on Tía Nona? "Papi said the cheese has protein, remember?"

Gracie smirked. "Yeah, whatever."

I was about to say something else to defend Tía Nona, but then I remembered, pizza's a good thing. So why were we all talking like it wasn't? That Gracie just got me all turned around sometimes.

Chapter 11

M Y PARENTS LET ME SKIP CHURCH on Sunday so I could go to the Cloisters with Tía Nona. Mami wasn't all that happy about it, though. "Don't you want to go too?" she asked Gracie about a million times.

But Gracie was eager to be rid of Tía Nona for a day. "No, no, no," she said. "You know museums are Anamay's thing. I'll be bored to death if I go."

Juan Miguel had some business meeting, so he dropped Tía Nona off at our building and continued in the taxicab, saying he would come back around dinnertime. Tía Nona and I waited in the lobby for Ruben and Claudia. Ruben's mom walked him over. "You behave yourself," she told him as she straightened out the collar on his polo shirt and ran her fingers through his curls.

"Stop it!" Ruben backed away from his mom and frowned.

"I gave him money for lunch and a souvenir," Mrs. Rivera said to Tía Nona.

"Oh, no, he's our guest," my aunt said. "I'll take care of everything."

"That's very generous of you," Mrs. Rivera said. "But it doesn't surprise me that Mecho's sister would be so sweet."

Tía Nona and Mrs. Rivera were best friends by the time Claudia arrived. She jumped out of her mom's car and rushed toward my building. She turned around and waved when she reached the glass door to the lobby. Her mom sped away. She never parked her car in our neighborhood because she was afraid it might get stolen.

"It's so great to meet Anamay's friends!" Tía Nona said after Mrs. Rivera left. "I'll bet you're both smart and talented, just like my niece."

"Ruben's the youngest kid in our grade at school," I said as we walked out the door. "He started school early because he learned to read when he was three."

"Impressive," Tía Nona said. Ruben blushed.

"And Claudia's going to be a singer-songwriter when she grows up. She's already published a few poems." Then I told Claudia in English what I had just said.

"I understood you," Claudia said. She smiled and nudged me with her elbow.

"Oh, sorry." Whenever Claudia's parents spoke to her in Spanish, she answered in English. And I always had to translate for her whenever Mami said anything because Claudia insisted Mami spoke way too fast. But she actually tried to speak Spanish as we walked with my aunt, and she was pretty good. By the time we arrived at the Cloisters twenty minutes later, I swear she was almost fluent.

Of course, Tía Nona wanted to practice her English too, so all day we went back and forth speaking in both languages. It was like talking with my sisters, except way more interesting. At the museum, Tía Nona explained the artwork to us. During lunch, she told us about Madrid and some of her other trips, while I ate a delicious club sandwich with french fries. (Not real food, according to Mami.) It was the best day ever, until Claudia mentioned the Eleanor School.

"Did Anamay tell you she might go to my school for eighth grade?" she asked my aunt.

"Yes, and it sounds like a wonderful opportunity." Tía Nona turned to Ruben. "Are you going to apply for a scholarship there too?"

Ruben shook his head. "My mom doesn't want me to go to school with a bunch of rich snobs." He looked at Claudia and quickly added, "No offense."

But how could she not be offended? I would be, if someone called me a rich snob. So, of course, Claudia was too. She crossed her arms over her chest and frowned at Ruben.

"Does anyone want dessert?" Tía Nona said in a super cheerful voice.

"The chocolate cake looks good," I said. Then we had a way-too-long conversation about dessert, just Tía Nona and me. When the waitress came, Claudia glanced at the menu and right away ordered the raspberry sorbet. Then she snapped the menu shut and glared at Ruben. He wouldn't look at her.

"I'll have the vanilla ice cream," he said to the waitress. "No fancy desserts for me." Then he clinked the ice cubes in his glass of cola until the server came over with our food. It was a long few minutes, with Ruben clinking, Claudia glaring, and Tía Nona chattering away about sweets from around the world while she glanced back and forth between the two of them.

After lunch, we waited outside the restaurant until Claudia's mom came to pick her up. "Can't I go spend the night at Anamay's?" Claudia asked. She already had a toothbrush and extra underwear at my house, just in case. I had the same at her house. But even though Claudia had her own room with two big beds in it, she preferred to stay in a sleeping bag on the floor in my house.

"No, sweetie," Claudia's mom said. "We need to get you packed up for camp."

Claudia groaned, then hugged me and Tía Nona goodbye. "See you around, Ruben," she mumbled.

"Bye," Ruben said. He still wouldn't look at her.

Tía Nona's phone rang as we were walking back to our apartment building. "It's Juan Miguel," she said. "You kids walk ahead. I'll catch up." She fell a few steps behind.

"Why were you so rude to Claudia?" I said to Ruben.

"I'm sorry," he said. "I just don't want you to go to a different school."

"We'll still see each other," I said. "We live two blocks apart. Plus we'll hang out at the library and after church."

Ruben kicked a pebble up the hill toward my house. "I know, but still."

"You know I can only go to Eleanor if I get a full scholarship," I said. "That might not happen."

Ruben looked up at me and smiled. "Well, you can always go to Science."

I shook my head. "I'm worried. I mean, what if I don't get into Eleanor *or* Science?"

"Why would you think that?" Ruben said.

"You remember what your mom told us," I said.

As the head librarian of our local public library, Mrs. Rivera followed a lot of kids' educations. "Back when I was your age," she told Ruben and me one day, "we just woke up on a Saturday morning, hopped on the subway, and walked in to take the test for Science. The smarter kids got in, and that was that. Now people with money hire tutors and enroll their children in prep courses. It's getting harder and harder for our kids from Washington Heights to get accepted." So she planned to hire a tutor for Ruben even though she didn't have a whole lot of money. Like Claudia, Ruben was an only child. But my parents didn't get a tutor for Gracie, so of course they probably wouldn't do it for me either.

"Don't worry," Ruben said. "You're the smartest person I know. If you can't get in, nobody can."

I smiled. "I hope you're right."

"I know I am," Ruben said. He focused on his pebble again. "I don't think Claudia's a snob or anything. And I know you won't become one either. It's just that I'll miss you."

"I know. I'll miss you too."

There wasn't anything more to say, so we didn't. We just walked with our arms looped together, Ruben kicking his pebble. People walking past us probably thought he was my little brother. Mami always told me not to get used to being taller than Ruben. "Boys shoot up in high school," she said. "Before you know it, you'll be craning your neck to look at him."

Maybe she was right, but for now, when I looked at him, I wondered: If I did have a little brother, would he be like Ruben? If he was, I'd be okay with that.

Chapter 12

CLAUDIA CALLED TUESDAY MORNING TO SAY goodbye. "How long will you be gone?" I asked.

"Four weeks."

"Which camp is this?" Claudia spent her summers at three different sleepaway camps, and I could never keep track of them.

"The camping and hiking one, so no telephones allowed," she said. "Now tell me about your Lincoln Center plans!"

"Ugh," I said. "I don't have any."

"Really? Doña Dulce hasn't told you yet whether you're going?"

"Nope. I have a lesson at three o'clock today. She probably wants to break the bad news in person."

"Orrrrr," Claudia said, stretching out the *r* so it sounded like an echo, "she wants to tell you the *good* news in person." Classic Claudia, always looking on the bright side. I didn't want to get my hopes up. "You have to write to let me know,

71

okay?" She gave me her address at camp. "You also have to tell me about your Eleanor visit."

The Eleanor School was having an information session and tour for students whose schools had recommended them for the scholarship test. It was on a Saturday, and my whole family was going, just like we all went to the Little Bethlehem open house for Gracie last year.

"My dad is honking the horn at me, so I'd better go," Claudia said. "I'll see you next month! Don't forget to write!"

The phone clicked to silence before I got a chance to say goodbye. I hung up and went to the piano. I needed to practice if I wanted to impress Doña Dulce at my lesson that afternoon, just in case she had anything to do with picking who played at Lincoln Center. I took my books out of the bench. As soon as I sat down, Rosie plopped herself on the couch and turned on the television.

"Mami!" I called.

"What's the matter? Are you okay?" Mami rushed over from the bathroom.

"Rosie turned on the TV and I'm trying to practice," I said.

"But I'm bored," Rosie said.

Connie came over and pulled on Mami's blouse. "Look, they're growing," she said. She held up a tiny pot with a little green bud sprouting out of it. She and Mami had planted a bunch of flower seeds on the windowsill, and Connie checked them every day.

"Okay, let's go transfer these to the flower box on the balcony," Mami said. "Rosita, come help us."

"But I don't want to get my hands all muddy!" Rosie held her hands out like they were something special.

"Well, bring two of the pots and come sit with us while we plant." Mami went to the window, grabbed two little pots, and handed them to Rosie. She picked up four more, two in each hand. "Anamay, we'll get out of your hair now. Come on, girls."

"I wanted to watch TV," Rosie grumbled as she walked down the hall.

Finally, some peace and quiet. I set my timer to an hour and started with scales and finger exercises. According to Doña Dulce, these needed to be done every day no matter what. Then I opened the Clementi book to my favorite sonatina. I had just learned it a few weeks earlier, but it was sounding pretty good. I clicked on the metronome. Last week Doña Dulce told me to forget the metronome and just play from the heart. But what did that even mean? After all, piano is like math. There is one right way that a piece of music should sound, and you have to concentrate and get it right. I practiced and practiced. I sped up the metronome a little bit at a time, until the tempo was perfect and I didn't miss a single note.

I was surprised when the timer buzzed. Usually my practice time was cut short by one interruption or another, but I actually got in a whole hour that day. Still, it felt like I had been playing for only a few minutes.

73

But not to my little sisters. They tumbled into the living room as soon as the timer went off. Before I had put all my books away, the television was back on and the room was full of noise. I went to my room and read until it was time to go to Doña Dulce's.

* * *

I ran all the way home after my piano lesson. The whole time I thought of ways to break the news to my family. *Guess what, Gracie? You have a dress to make!* No, that was silly. Maybe I could pretend I was sad, and then spring it on them like an April Fools' Day joke. No, that would be weird. Plus I couldn't seem to stop smiling, so my face would be a dead giveaway. Okay then, I would just walk in the door and smile. They would all know right away.

I opened the door, beaming. But nobody was thinking about me and Lincoln Center. They didn't even notice when I walked in. Instead, Abuelita was telling Tía Nona and Juan Miguel that Tío Lalo could drive them to the airport the next day.

"That's okay, Mamá," Tía Nona said. "We don't want to bother him, with his new job and everything. We'll just take a cab."

"But he said it's no problem at all," Abuelita said. "And he already has the day off."

"Really?" Mami said. "Why? Did he get fired again?"

Abuelita gave Mami the evil eye and stamped her foot.

"No! He's off every Wednesday." She turned away like she couldn't stand to look at Mami for one more second.

"Well . . . but . . ." Tía Nona looked at Mami, then at Juan Miguel, then back at Mami. Mami bit her lower lip and studied the floor.

"I'm sure Lalo would rather do something fun on his day off," Juan Miguel said. "We don't want to be a bother."

"But I'm telling you it's no bother! Not at all. He loves his sister, and he wants to do this for you."

"Okay, we'll call him when we get back to the hotel tonight," Tía Nona said.

I knew she wouldn't call him. But the conversation seemed to be over, so I walked over to the couch and sat on the arm next to Mami. "Guess what?" I said.

"Just a minute, Anamay," Abuelita said. "Here, Nona, let me write down Lalo's number for you. Mecho, do you have a pen and paper?"

"I'll just put it in my phone," Tía Nona said. She took out her cell phone.

"How do you do that?" Abuelita walked over and stood next to Tía Nona, staring down at the cell phone.

I could not believe this. Mami knew I had just come back from my piano lesson. Why didn't she ask me about Lincoln Center? And did Abuelita really need to learn how to save numbers in a cell phone *right now*?

Papi walked in the door. Surely he would want to hear my news. "Guess what?" I said again.

"You *are* going to call him, right?" Abuelita was yelling now.

Tía Nona didn't look up from her phone. "Yes, of course," she said softly.

Juan Miguel and Mami looked at each other with raised eyebrows.

"Call who?" Papi asked.

"Lalo," Abuelita said. "He's taking them to the airport tomorrow. He just bought a car, you know."

"Oh," Papi said.

"What? Do you think that's a problem?" Abuelita stood there with her hands on her hips, ready for a fight.

"Well . . ." Papi looked at Mami, then Tía Nona, then Juan Miguel. "Yes, as a matter of fact I do."

Everybody gasped. Or maybe it was just me.

"Why? Why is that a problem?!" A vein throbbed on Abuelita's forehead.

Papi closed his eyes for a second. "Look," he said, "Lalo is a loving son, brother, and uncle. He's a lot of fun to be with, and I know he's a very good person."

Okay, that was a good beginning. Abuelita still looked upset, though. Like the rest of us, she knew the "but" was coming.

"But," Papi said, "he drinks too much, and driving drunk is illegal and dangerous. It's only a matter of time before he kills someone."

I couldn't believe Papi had come right out and said that.

Neither could anyone else. Mami, Tía Nona, and Juan Miguel looked at him with their mouths open, probably in awe. After all, they were all thinking the same thing but hadn't dared to say it.

After a moment of silence in the room, Abuelita chuckled and waved her arm at Papi like she was shooing away a pesky fly. "Oh, Tavito, lighten up. You worry too much." She turned to Tía Nona. "You will call him, right?"

"I'll call him to say goodbye," Tía Nona said. "But I agree with Tavito. It's not safe for Lalo to drive."

Abuelita stood there like a statue and stared at Tía Nona for a long time. At least it felt like a long time, and it was super awkward. Thank goodness for Connie. She picked that exact moment to wake up from her nap and run into the living room. "Abuelita!" Connie dove into Abuelita with her arms open.

"Oh, my goodness, who is this big girl?" Abuelita sat and lifted Connie onto her lap.

"Sing the song about the *palomita*," Connie bossed, as usual.

"Okay." Abuelita cleared her throat. "*Ay, mi palomita, la que yo adoré . . .*"

Rosie and Tía Nona followed Mami into the kitchen to get dinner ready. Gracie snuck off to our room to use the cell phone she just got as a graduation present, and Papi and Juan Miguel started talking baseball. Nobody asked me about the Winter Showcase.

I went to my parents' room and wrote a letter to Claudia. At least I could tell *her* my news.

Chapter 13

THAT NIGHT I DREAMT I WAS performing at Lincoln Center. My fingers flew over the keys of a shiny grand piano, playing Chopin's Polonaise in G Minor perfectly. My heart pounded with excitement and my face flushed with joy. When I finished my piece, the audience went wild, clapping and cheering. I looked down at them and I didn't see a single familiar face. Then I remembered that my family didn't even know I was there. My brilliant performance didn't feel so joyous anymore. I stood up slowly to take a bow. That's when I noticed I wasn't wearing any clothes. Of course, Mami and Gracie hadn't known to make me a dress. The people in the audience pointed and laughed. Eleanor's head of school laughed louder than anyone else.

I just stood there, my hands over my face, and cried.

"Anamay."

Who was calling my name? Did someone in the crowd actually know me?

"Anamay!"

I opened my eyes and blinked.

"Anamay." The voice wasn't in my dream. I rubbed my eyes and looked up. Gracie was looking down from the top bunk, her hair dangling toward me and her phone beaming in her hand. She pulled the buds out of her ears. "Anamay," she said again. "Are you awake?"

"I am now," I said grumpily. But I was glad she had gotten me out of that nightmare. I reached into the drawer under my bed and pulled out my glasses. If Gracie was going to chat, I wanted to look at her and see more than a blur.

"I was watching a video on YouTube," she said. "This girl was playing piano, and I thought about you and Lincoln Center. Did Doña Dulce say anything? You never told us."

Well, of course I didn't, because nobody asked. And I was still kind of mad about it. But Gracie was asking now, and that made my heart jump a little. And then I jumped up too, and that smile came back on my face.

Gracie hopped down and lunged at me, laughing and saying, "I knew it! I knew it!" Her squeals woke up Rosie, who came over and joined Gracie and me on my bed.

"Tell us everything," Gracie said. "From the minute you walked into Doña Dulce's house until the minute she told you." She sat cross-legged across from me. The night-light behind her glowed like a halo.

"Well," I said. I crossed my legs too, and Rosie leaned up against me. "Let me see. First Doña Dulce's husband answered the door, and he didn't act any different than usual. And I could hear Sarita playing in the front room, just like always. So I thought, okay, I'm definitely not going."

Rosie giggled. "He was just being sneaky, right?"

"I guess so," I said. "And so was Doña Dulce. She told me to sit down and start with a few scales, like it was a regular old lesson."

Gracie shook her head. "Typical."

"Then, while I was in the middle of an arpeggio, she started to fumble through a bunch of papers, and I got annoyed, because she wasn't even listening to me!" I sucked in a big breath. My sisters didn't take their eyes off of me. "All of a sudden, she yelled out, 'Aha!' and I stopped playing. I looked at her, and she waved a letter in her hand and said, 'Ana María, please help me. I got this letter in English and I need you to read it to me.' So I took the paper, and the first thing I saw was my name right there in the middle. And Sarita's name too. So then, of course, I knew."

"Did you read the letter to her?" Rosie was sitting straight up now.

"Yes," I said. "But I could tell she already knew what it said. She just sat there with a big old smile on her face the whole time I was reading. And when I got to my name, she clapped and gave me a big hug. Then Mr. Sánchez came in with a tray of cookies and soda, and he went and got Sarita, and we all celebrated."

"What did the letter say?" Rosie asked.

I looked up and studied the underside of the top bunk, like I was thinking hard to remember. But actually, I had memorized every word. "Well, it said: *Dear Mrs. Sánchez, Thank you for your interest in participating in our Winter Showcase. After careful consideration, we are pleased to inform you that we have selected the following two students to represent your piano school this year—*"

"They called it a school?" Gracie said.

"Yep, that's exactly what it said."

"So then it was your name and Sarita's too?" Rosie asked. I nodded.

"Did the letter say anything else?" Rosie was very interested in this letter.

"Yes, it had a bunch of information about the date and the time and that sort of thing. So, the showcase is on the Sunday before Christmas, at two o'clock."

"Oh, this is so exciting!" Gracie said. She hugged me so tight I could hardly breathe. As soon as she let go, Rosie threw herself at me.

"Does this mean you're famous now, Anamay?" Rosie asked.

"No, you silly goose. It's just a kids' recital."

"But it's a big deal," Gracie said. "So you might get famous one day."

The three of us sat there giggling and talking about me being famous and what we should wear to the recital. Rosie was happy to hear she had to dress up too. And when Gracie told her it would be too cold to wear the dress Tía Nona had just bought for her, Rosie got super excited. "I'll get another new dress!" She bounced on the bed.

We had so much to say that we forgot it was the middle of the night—until we noticed Mami standing in the doorway.

"Excuse me, girls," Mami said. "Do you realize what time it is?"

"But, Mami, Anamay got picked to go to Lincoln Center!" Gracie said. "And nobody even asked her about it all day!"

Mami opened her mouth and put her hands on her cheeks. "Oh, *mamita*, I'm so sorry." She walked over, grabbed my face, and kissed my cheeks over and over. "I'm so proud of you, *mi amor*. We have to tell your father." She left the room, but came right back with Papi behind her. Connie was wide awake and getting a piggyback ride from him.

"This calls for a celebration!" Papi said. "To the kitchen!"

"But don't you have to get up early for work tomorrow?" I said. "And we don't want to disturb the neighbors, right?"

"It's okay if I'm tired at work for one day," Papi said. "And we can celebrate quietly. How about some ice cream?"

"Yay!" we all screamed.

Mami put her finger on her lips and said, "Shh."

We put our hands over our mouths and said "Yay" again, but in a whisper this time. We giggled all the way to the kitchen. Claudia always said I was lucky to have sisters. Maybe she was right.

Chapter 14

I SLEPT INTO THE MORNING WITHOUT ANY more dreams. When I opened my eyes, the sun poured in over the top of the drawn curtains, telling me that the day had started hours ago. I took out my glasses and put them on. Rosie was sound asleep, her knees tucked under her belly and her bottom pointed up in the air. A little drool had dribbled out of her open mouth and onto her pillow. I pulled back my covers and ducked under Gracie's dangling arm to get out of bed.

Mami and Abuelita were talking in the kitchen. Abuelita would surely lecture me about "the importance of always looking your best" if I went out there in my pajamas. So I picked out some clothes and went to the bathroom to scrub myself clean and try to brush the frizz out of my hair.

Abuelita jumped up and hugged me when I walked into the kitchen. "The concert pianist is here!"

I smiled. "It's not that big a deal," I said. "It's just a kids' recital."

Mami put her hand on my shoulder. "Stop being so modest, Anamay," she said. "You've worked hard for this, and you deserve some fuss. Now, come have breakfast." Mami forked out a steaming boiled plantain from a pot on the stove and put it on a plate. "What do you want with your *mangú*?" she asked as she mashed the plantain with the fork.

"Um, could I have fried cheese?" I asked.

"Of course. Take it out of the refrigerator and slice up however much you want."

The cheese was sizzling in the pan when Gracie came in. "You know," she said, "we need to start thinking about a dress for Anamay's recital."

"I agree," Mami said. "We can pick out a pattern now, but the annual sale at Cristina's isn't until October. We'll buy the material then."

Cristina's Fabrics was Mami's favorite place, and Gracie's too. When Mami and Gracie talked about sewing, they acted like nobody else was in the room. It was the same thing with Mami and Rosie in the kitchen together. And when Mami showed Connie how to repot a plant that had outgrown its first home, there was no talking to either one of them. They just didn't notice you. But the worst was the sewing, because Gracie and Mami always sewed for someone else. And if you were the one getting a new outfit, it was like you were just a mannequin. I was glad about playing at Lincoln Center and getting a chance to impress some people from the Eleanor School, but I was not looking forward to this whole dress-making process.

✳ ✳ ✳

The next day Abuelita rode the two subway stops with us to Cristina's. We walked straight to the table with all the pattern books on it. Rosie sat between Mami and Abuelita, and Connie climbed onto Mami's lap. Gracie and I sat across from them with the Vogue pattern book in front of us. "Vogue is the fanciest," Gracie said. She turned to the evening wear pages.

"Those dresses are too grown-up for Anamay," Mami said. "Check the children's section." She pointed to a babyish dress in the book in front of her. "Look, isn't this adorable?"

Abuelita leaned over Rosie and studied the dress Mami had picked out. "Oh, yes, that's darling," she said.

"No, no, no," Gracie said. "She needs a long gown. Those little-girl dresses won't work."

"She's only eleven years old," Mami said. "She is not wearing that dress with the back all exposed. It's not appropriate."

"She'll be twelve by the time of the concert," Gracie said.

Mami cocked her head to one side and gave Gracie a do-you-think-I'm-stupid look. "Anamay is not wearing any of those mature-looking dresses."

Gracie huffed and slammed the book shut, then reached for another one. Again, she went to the evening wear pages.

"This book has prom dresses for high school girls. Anamay's almost in high school." She pointed at one dress and turned the book around so Mami could see. "What about this?"

Mami took the book from Gracie. "Hmm, that is nice. What do you think, Mamá?"

Abuelita examined the page. "That's perfect," she said. "Very suitable for a girl Anamay's age."

I cleared my throat loudly. "Do I get an opinion here?"

Mami looked at me like she was surprised I was there. "Oh, of course, *mamita*." She handed the book to me. "Do you like this?"

I was sure I wouldn't, and then I'd make them watch me go through every single book until I picked out the perfect dress. The perfect dress for me. Not them. That would serve them right. I put the book down in front of me and looked at the dress Gracie had picked out. It had a lace top and sleeves. The skirt gathered at the waist, then fluttered down to the ground, giving me enough room to work the pedals. It was beautiful.

"Can I get it in red?" I said.

Chapter 15

THE TELEPHONE WAS RINGING WHEN WE got home. It was Mami's friend Millie. "Millie's baby is sick," Mami said when she hung up. "I'm going to babysit Max so she can take the baby to the emergency room."

"Now?" Gracie said.

"Yes. Let's Max-proof the house. You know how he is."

"We all know how he is," I said. Millie was nice enough, but people in the neighborhood ran away screaming when they saw four-year-old Max coming.

"Oh no, not Max!" Rosie slapped herself on the forehead. "He drives me crazy."

Gracie laughed. "You've been crazy for a long time, missy," she said. "Max has nothing to do with it."

"But he wants to play tag all the time. ALL. THE. TIME. I mean, what's wrong with sitting and relaxing? He's exhausting!" Rosie plopped herself down on the living room floor and spread her arms.

"Max is fun!" Connie jumped and jumped.

"I need to practice piano," I said. "Mami, do I have time before things get crazy?"

"Millie said she'll be here in fifteen minutes, so you'd better hurry."

I went to the piano bench and pulled out two finger exercise books. I sat down and started with some scales.

"Put these in my room," Mami said.

I turned my head and saw Gracie pick up the vase of silk flowers from the coffee table. I messed up and skipped an F-sharp. I started over.

"What about these?" Rosie said.

"Oh, yes, put that in my room too," Mami said.

I peeked again. Rosie was skipping down the hallway with a picture frame in each hand, while Connie followed behind her, holding two more frames. I remembered the F-sharp this time, but not the C-sharp. I grunted and started again. This was getting annoying.

My sisters came back to the living room. "I put the toothpaste on the highest shelf," Gracie said.

"Good thinking," Mami said. The last time Max was at our house, he squeezed a whole tube of toothpaste all over the floor.

I decided I had had enough of scales. I opened Hanon's *The Virtuoso Pianist in Sixty Exercises for the Piano*. I had just finished the first exercise when Millie knocked on the door.

Max burst in with a navy-blue towel tied around his neck and flowing down his back. He jumped onto the couch and yelled, "I'm Superman!"

Rosie and Connie gasped. "No jumping on the couch!" Connie shouted.

"But I'm Superman!"

"Jumping isn't allowed," Rosie said. "We're not animals!"

I kept playing as I listened to Millie outside the door, thanking Mami and explaining about the baby's fever and stuff. "Maxito, stop!" she screamed. "Sit down like a civilized person!"

"It's okay," Mami said. "He's just excited. He'll settle down as soon as you leave. Now don't worry about a thing and take your time coming back for him."

Why was Mami lying? She knew Max would never settle down. I clicked on the metronome and tried to tune out the noise behind me.

"Let's play tag!" Max yelled.

The metronome was not enough to drown out the arguing about who would be "it." I counted out loud. Very loud. "One-two-three-four-one-two-three-four."

Thumps and laughter behind me. Then a scream. It was Connie. "That's my Barbie! Put her down!"

"Max, give it back to her," Gracie said.

"One-two-three-four."

"Noooo!" Connie yelled. "You broke her! Mami, he broke her!"

"Max, you tore her head off!" Mami said. "That wasn't very nice."

"One-two-three-four."

Connie cried and cried.

"Anamay can fix it later, *mamita*," Mami said. "She's good at these things. For now, your Barbie will rest on top of the refrigerator."

"One-two-three-four-one-two-three-four." Suddenly, I felt a blow to the back of my head. I turned around. Max was being an airplane and running around the room with his arms out wide. He had smacked me when he whizzed by.

"That's it," I said. "I give up." I stood up and tossed my piano books back into the bench. Then I walked down the hall without looking back.

"Anamay, help us entertain him," Gracie called.

I went into my room and closed the door. I felt a little guilty about abandoning my sisters. But this was all Mami's fault. She agreed to babysit her friend's savage kid when she knew I needed to practice. Thanks to her, I would never be as good as Sarita, and I would probably embarrass myself at Lincoln Center with Eleanor's head of school watching! Let Mami deal with Max. I had to work on my scholarship application and study for the test. I was definitely going to need a perfect score now.

Chapter 16

PAPI STAYED HOME FROM WORK THE next day to go to the doctor with Mami.

"Is Mami sick?" Connie asked.

"No," Papi said. "She and the baby just need a checkup. Like the one you had a few months ago, remember?"

"Is the baby getting a shot?"

Papi chuckled. "No, not today. But Mami is, and she'll be a little tired when she gets home, so she won't be able to carry you."

Connie crossed her arms and lifted her chin in the air. "She doesn't have to carry me," she said. "I'm a big girl."

"Well, of course you are," Papi said. "But is it okay if I pick you up now and give you a big hug?"

Connie tilted her head and looked at the ceiling. "Well . . . okay." Then she jumped into his arms.

"What is this shot you're getting?" I asked Mami.

"It's just a little test," Mami said. "To make sure everything's fine."

"Why wouldn't everything be fine?" I said. "Are you sick?" Could Max have made Mami sick? I did hear him cough a few times. That beast never even covered his mouth. Maybe this was my fault for not helping out yesterday.

"Stop worrying, Anamay," Mami said. "I'm not sick. This is just a precaution. Now, you two"—she pointed at Gracie and me—"take good care of your sisters, don't leave the house, and don't let anyone come in while we're out."

Gracie and I nodded.

"We'll be back in a few hours." Mami gave each of us a hug and a kiss and walked out the door with Papi.

"Anamay, will you fix my Barbie now?"

Poor Connie. She had cried herself to sleep last night. Max was still at our house when Connie went to bed. He napped on the couch until his mother finally came back. Mami didn't want to take the doll down before Max left. Just in case.

"Of course, *mamita*," I said. I went into the kitchen and found Barbie's body and her severed head. Then I sat down to work while Connie stood beside me. She leaned in close, her warm breath smelling like orange juice against my cheek. I squeezed the doll's head to widen the neck hole, and then I pushed the bulb of the neck into the opening. It went in pretty easily, but I twisted the head a few times to make sure it was on there good and tight. "Here you go," I said as I handed the doll to Connie.

Connie grabbed Barbie and hugged her. "Thank you, thank you!" she said. Then she threw her arms around me. It was nice to see Connie so happy. I picked her up and hugged her back. "Will you read to us now?" she asked.

"Sure, what do you want to read?"

Connie ran around the apartment and gathered up every picture book in the place. "What are you doing?" Rosie asked her.

"Finding books for Anamay to read to me."

"Oh, can I help?" Rosie didn't wait for an answer. Before I knew it, there were eighteen books piled on the coffee table.

I sat on the couch with one little sister on each side of me. "Let's start with the library books," I said. "Since we have to take them back soon."

"Where's Gracie?" Rosie asked. "Doesn't she want to read with us?"

I shrugged. "She's probably on her phone or something." I opened the first book.

"Oh, can I read it?" Rosie said. She leaned on my arm.

"Sure," I said. Connie leaned on my other arm, and she propped up her doll so it was facing the book. Rosie started to read. Both my sisters' heads blocked my view of the book, but that was okay. I knew all these books by heart.

Gracie came into the living room when Rosie was on the last page. She was wearing lipstick and a white tank top, and she had rolled up the elastic waistband on her red shorts to make them even shorter. She waited for Rosie to finish.

"I'm going out," Gracie said. "I'll be right back."

"Where are you going?" I asked. "And whose lipstick is that? You're not allowed to use makeup."

Gracie rolled her eyes. "I'm just going down to the lobby," she said.

"Oh, is Pedro meeting you downstairs?" Rosie stretched out the first syllable in "Pedro" and made kissing noises.

Gracie chuckled. "Maybe," she said. "But only for a minute."

It was more than a minute. It was fourteen books later. And when she came back, she washed off the lipstick, unrolled her shorts, and sat down to read with us like nothing had happened. Like she hadn't disobeyed Mami. Like she just knew no one would tell on her.

* * *

Papi was right about Mami being tired after her appointment. She went straight to bed when they got home. Then Papi went out and brought back two pizzas for dinner. Pizza again? And without salad this time? Maybe this was my lucky week.

We sat at the table and opened the first box. "Don't tell your mother I got pepperoni," Papi said with a wink. "She'd have a fit if she knew." He took a bite, then looked around the table at my sisters and me. "So, what did you girls do while we were out?"

Gracie answered right away. "We read a bunch of books," she said. "See the pile on the table?"

"And I read most of them," Rosie said.

Papi raised his eyebrows and nodded. "Impressive," he said.

"And Anamay fixed my Barbie." Connie held the doll up for Papi to see.

"You're not supposed to bring Barbie to the dinner table," Gracie said. "You might get her clothes dirty."

"Oh, really," I said. "Since when do you care about doing what you're supposed to?"

Gracie looked at me with wide-open eyes. I swear she stopped breathing.

"What do you mean by that?" Papi said. He looked back and forth between Gracie and me while he chewed. "Did something happen today?"

Gracie looked like she would cry. Her eyes stayed on mine, and I could tell what she was thinking: *Please, please, please don't tell.*

I looked at Papi. What would he do if I told him that Gracie had put on makeup and super short shorts to be alone with a boy? Would he make too big a deal out of it? Would he ground Gracie for life? Would she hate me for life?

"She only read with us the last few books," I said. "Other than that, I was on my own with Connie and Rosie. I think she was on her phone." I couldn't believe I had lied. But it wasn't really a lie, I told myself, because she probably was on her phone at first. She had definitely spoken with Pedro before she met him in the lobby, right?

"Well, I guess you deserved that," Papi said. "Since you left her alone to deal with Max last night."

"That's different," I said. "Mami was here yesterday, and she was in charge."

"Anamay's right," Gracie said quickly. "Mami left both of us to take care of Connie and Rosie, and I should have helped more." She looked me in the eyes. "I'm sorry, Anamay. It won't happen again. And thank you for picking up the slack for me."

"Oh no!" Connie yelled. She held up her Barbie with pizza sauce all over her fingers. "Her clothes are dirty now!"

Papi and I shook our heads. Gracie jumped up. "Come on, let's wash that out before it stains." She took Connie's hand and dragged her to the bathroom. More importantly, she got herself out of there before Connie or Rosie could let the truth slip out. I shook my head again. That Gracie was pretty clever sometimes.

Chapter 17

As usual, a swarm of people followed us home after Mass on Sunday. Gracie was super happy when Mami invited Pedro and his mother too. At home, Mami went straight to the kitchen and got out a loaf of bread and a bunch of cans of deviled ham. Rosie stood on her stool and smoothed a thin layer of ham on slice after slice of bread. She handed each finished slice to Gracie, who covered it with another slice and cut the sandwiches into four triangles. Mami arranged the pieces neatly on a long platter.

"Can I take these out to everyone?" Gracie asked.

"Yes," Mami said. "And help Abuelita entertain our guests."

Gracie grabbed the platter and ran into the living room with a big smile on her face.

Papi stood guard over the coffeepot, waiting to pour as soon as the coffee was done. I took the tiny coffee cups out and arranged them on two trays, five cups on each tray, with a little bowl of sugar in the middle. After Papi poured the coffee, Mami took the first tray, and I waited for the second one.

"You go ahead, Ana María," Papi said. "I'll take the rest of the coffee out."

All the seats were taken in the living room. Connie was on Abuelita's lap, and my grandmother's friend, Doña Paula, sat next to them on the couch, talking about her aches and pains. Pedro's mom sat on the other side of Doña Paula with her hand over her mouth to cover her yawns. Gracie and Pedro were on the floor making googly eyes at each other. Mrs. Rivera was showing Rosie some new books she had in her bag. Ruben says his mom never takes a day off from being a librarian. That made sense to me. Why would anyone want a day off from books?

"Hey, Anamay," Ruben said. "I brought a new puzzle." He took a box with an autumn landscape on it out of his mother's bag. "It's five hundred pieces, for ages twelve and up."

Ruben and I like to challenge ourselves. If a puzzle says it's for our age group, we skip it. Too babyish for us. We sat at the dining room table and started with the edge pieces of the puzzle. It's the only way to do it.

Papi walked into the kitchen and Mr. Jiménez followed behind him. "I don't understand these papers I got from the government," Mr. Jiménez said.

Papi took the stack of crumpled papers and looked them over. "These aren't from the government," he said. "They're from your landlord. Have you paid your rent?"

Ruben handed me an orange puzzle piece. "This one goes on your side," he said.

I took the piece and gave him a blue one. "This one must be the sky," I said.

"Let's separate out the pieces by color," he said. "That'll make it easier to figure out where everything goes."

"Good idea." Ruben and I concentrated on our puzzle. Around us, Papi translated the letter for Mr. Jiménez, Doña Paula and Abuelita gave Mami advice about something related to babies, and Mrs. Rivera read to Rosie and Connie. Mr. Jiménez's baby let out a loud squeal, and Mrs. Jiménez walked around the living room bouncing the baby on her shoulder. Doña Paula's son and his friend got into an argument over which was the better team, the Yankees or the Mets. It was a typical Sunday at our house.

"Where's Altagracia?" Papi asked.

I looked over to where I had seen Gracie sitting with Pedro before, but they weren't there. Papi marched down the hall toward the bedroom.

"What's going on in here?" He was probably at the door to our bedroom, but his voice carried all the way down to the rest of us. Even the baby got quiet.

"We'd better finish this puzzle fast," Ruben said. "I get the feeling this party will be over soon."

I could hear Gracie crying. "We were just talking," she said. "It was too noisy in the living room."

"Come out here right now," Papi said.

Pedro's mom jumped up and disappeared down the hallway. She dragged Pedro into the living room by the ear as Gracie and Papi followed behind them. "I'm so sorry," she said to Mami and Papi. "This will never happen again. I'll talk to him at home." She was still holding Pedro's ear when they walked out the door.

"This certainly won't happen again," Papi said to Gracie, "because that young man is never coming into this house again. And you, young lady, are not going out for a month!"

Gracie's face was all teary. "I said we were just talking! Why do you make such a big deal out of everything? You're ruining my life!" She stomped back to our room and slammed the door.

"I'm sorry about this," Papi said to everyone.

"Oh, believe me," Doña Paula said. "I understand the teenage years." She went into a long, embarrassing story about something her son had done as a teenager. He kept interrupting to defend himself, and everyone else laughed.

"Do you want to go talk to her?" Ruben said to me.

"Huh? Who?"

"Your sister. Do you want to go cheer her up?"

"No, she'll be fine." I put a puzzle piece in its place. We were doing a good job, and we couldn't stop now. Besides, Gracie didn't need me, right? I wouldn't even know what to say.

Chapter 18

EVERYTHING STARTED GOING MY WAY ONCE Gracie was grounded. First, she wasn't allowed to go to some Fourth of July party at her friend's house. That meant Mami and Papi stopped nagging me to go with her. Also, things got really quiet at home. Gracie moped around for a few days, not talking to anybody and looking all sad. Connie and Rosie and Mami stayed out of her way, tiptoeing around the place and speaking in soft voices. Even Chichi's twins were quiet when Mami babysat them two days in a row. This was perfect for practicing piano and studying for the Eleanor scholarship exam I would take in October. And I had a lot of work to do, especially on the piano.

"What would you like to play at Lincoln Center?" Doña Dulce asked at my lesson. "I'll need to notify the Piano Teachers' Association by September."

"Do I get to pick?" I said.

"Of course. I'll help you come up with an ideal piece

for you," she said. "But I want to know what moves you. Something soft and emotional, or something quick and powerful? Or something in between?"

What I really wanted was something that would impress the scholarship committee at the Eleanor School. But what would that be? "What's Sarita going to play?" I asked.

"Good question! You can't both play the same piece." Doña Dulce reached for a small notebook on top of the piano. She wet her thumb and forefinger with her tongue, and turned over a few pages. "Yes, here it is! We wrote down a few options and then settled on 'Jeux d'eau' by Maurice Ravel. It's a beautiful piece, and challenging even for Sarita."

Even for Sarita. It must be super hard, then.

"If you pick a piece now, you'll have five whole months to work on it. Would you like to try Chopin again?" Doña Dulce looked at me with hopeful eyes.

I wished I could play something contemporary with Claudia singing along like we always did when we got together. That would be fun. But maybe there was an impressive classical piece I could learn to love and play well too.

"If you want, you can choose a piece that is easy for you to master," Doña Dulce said. "You don't have to decide until September."

"No, no, I want to challenge myself like Sarita," I said slowly. I sort of meant it too. After all, I wanted to improve my playing and I also wanted to impress the Eleanor School.

But what if I did a lousy job? Would it be better for me to perform an easy piece flawlessly, or to play a super tough piece with a few mistakes? No, for a full scholarship I was going to need to play something difficult *and* play it perfectly. There was no other choice.

"Are you sure?" Doña Dulce asked.

I nodded.

"Good! Let's see what our choices are." She stood up and opened the top drawer of the black metal file cabinet next to her piano. "You have excellent rhythm," she said as she riffled through the books and sheet music in the drawer. "We should find something that utilizes that strength of yours." She plucked out some yellowed sheets held together by a paper clip and handed them to me. Then she turned back to the file cabinet and walked her fingers across the books that were packed into the second drawer.

I looked at the title page in my hand. "Meine Freuden" by Frédéric Chopin and Franz Liszt. This was definitely going to be tough if Chopin had to get help with it. I was afraid to turn to the first page.

"Okay." Doña Dulce sat down with two dog-eared books in her hands. "Here's a Chopin book and a Liszt book. Take a look at all of these, pull the songs up on YouTube, really listen and see how they make you feel. We have some time to choose your piece, so don't rush it. As far as practicing for now, let's stick with what you know, keeping your fingers limber and your sight reading sharp."

For the rest of the lesson, I played finger exercises and some pieces I already knew by heart, like "The Happy Farmer" and "Für Elise." The finger exercises were my favorites. Doña Dulce always marveled at what a great job I did on them. But with the songs, even the ones I thought were perfect, she always had something to say. "Loosen up! Use your heart, not your head!"

What did that even mean? I always used my head when I did things well. After all, there wasn't any other way, right?

Chapter 19

I WOKE UP SUPER EARLY ON SATURDAY. It was the day my family and I were going to the information session and tour at the Eleanor School. I was looking forward to seeing the school and learning all about the classes and activities. Also, I hoped to get some pointers about what it would take to get a full scholarship. By the time my parents and sisters woke up, I was already dressed.

After breakfast, the telephone rang and Mami answered it. I could tell it was bad news, especially when she said the words I hated: "Don't worry, we'll be right over." She turned to Gracie when she hung up. "Doña Paula's granddaughter is in a panic. Her wedding is this afternoon and the dog ripped off a piece of her dress. Let's go see what we can do to fix it."

"But . . . what about the Eleanor School?" I asked.

"*Ay, mamita*, I'm so sorry, but this is important. Besides, as long as *you* see the school and learn about it, that's all that matters, right?" Mami said.

"Don't worry, Ana María," Papi said. "There will be plenty of opportunities for your mother to see your new school when you're a student there."

I liked that Papi was talking as if I was definitely going to Eleanor, so I smiled and relaxed. "Sure, go fix the wedding dress."

Mami and Gracie left, and Papi went to put on a tie while I waited by the door with Connie and Rosie. I had told him he absolutely needed to wear a tie, which is why what happened next was all my fault. And what happened was that the telephone rang again.

"Hello?" I said.

"Hi, is this Gracie?"

"No."

"Anamay?"

"Yes?"

"This is Sarita."

"Oh, hi, Sarita." Why would Sarita call here? Did she have a piano question for me?

"I'm sorry to bother you, but I think my sister's having her baby soon, and my dad's at work, and I don't know what to do."

I looked at the clock on the wall. We had to leave right away to get to the information session on time. Besides, Papi wasn't a doctor. There was nothing he could do about this. "You should call 9-1-1," I said to Sarita. "They'll tell you what to do."

"Oh, okay . . ." Sarita's voice faded away. "Well, thank you," she said softly. Then she hung up.

I smiled as I put the phone down. I thought that went pretty well. In fact, I should probably always answer the phone from now on. I could figure out a way to get rid of each and every caller. My parents didn't understand that people could get by without them. They didn't need to stop what they were doing and get involved all the time. They just didn't realize that yet.

"Who was on the phone?" Papi reached for the door.

"Oh, it was just Sarita," I said in my breeziest voice. "She asked what to do if her sister was having the baby, so I told her to call 9-1-1." I started to walk out the door, like I knew no one would ever disagree with my advice.

"What?" Papi said. "Lucy's in labor?"

"Well, Sarita's not sure," I said. "That's why I told her to call 9-1-1. They could explain it to her, right?"

"Is her father home?" Papi asked.

I sighed. "No." I could feel my control of the situation slipping away. It was happening slowly, like the sand under your toes when you stand at the edge of the beach. You barely feel it, but it slides away from you a little at a time. Before you know it, you've lost your balance.

"What about her brothers?"

"What about them?" I asked.

"If Sarita goes to the hospital with Lucy, someone has to take care of her brothers," Papi said.

"Well, she has neighbors," I said. "Can't Doña Dulce watch them?"

Papi frowned. "I think we should go help them."

"But what about the information session?"

Papi put his hands on his hips and crinkled his eyebrows together. "I'll call the school on Monday and ask for a private tour."

I could not believe this. I blinked and blinked, and my breathing became heavy. "It won't be the same," I said. "There won't be presentations and I won't meet the other kids who would start with me."

Papi looked at me and sighed. "Ana María, I'm sorry, but our friends need us. I promise we'll figure out a way to see Eleanor soon." He yanked off the tie and walked out the door holding my sisters' hands.

I stood in the doorway for a few seconds, wondering if I should stay and work on my scholarship application. But what if we finished quickly with Lucy and Sarita? Or maybe they were already on their way to the hospital, and their brothers were safe and sound at a neighbor's house. The information session was scheduled to take a few hours, so maybe we could still catch most of it. I reached for Papi's tie, stuffed it in my pocket, and followed after him.

* * *

A screeching ambulance was inching its way down Sarita's street when we arrived. "This is ridiculous," Papi said.

"It has no place to stop with all those double-parked cars in the way."

When we got in the building, Papi pressed the elevator button. "That never works," I said.

"Oh, that's right, I forgot."

We started toward the stairs. Then a miracle happened: the elevator door opened. Rosie jumped inside and the rest of us followed. The door creaked as it closed slowly, and the elevator started to move just as slowly as the door. Rosie pushed the number 6 button over and over. "Does it know where to go?" she asked. The chunky wooden knobs were different from the buttons in the elevators in our building. Our buttons lit up when you pressed them.

"Yes," Papi said. "We'll get there eventually." But I could see that he was nervous. He held on to Connie tightly. When the elevator's hammering noises got extra loud, he told Rosie and me to grab the walls. Finally, the clanging stopped and the door creaked open. "Go ring their bell," Papi said to me. "I'll hold the elevator here so they can ride down."

Sarita was in tears when she answered the door. "The ambulance isn't here yet, and I don't know how Lucy's going to make it down the stairs."

"The elevator's working," I said. "My dad's holding the door for us."

Sarita squealed like she had just won the lottery. "Come on, Lucy, the elevator's working!"

Lucy hobbled over. She grabbed Sarita and groaned. Sweat ran down her face.

"Let's go, boys!" Sarita called. Her brothers zoomed out the door and almost knocked Lucy over.

Lucy moaned a lot in the elevator. This upset Connie, so soon she was sobbing. Papi held her in his arms and flinched every time Lucy cried out. He was probably thinking the same thing I was: *It sure would be good if Mami were here*. She would know how to help Lucy feel better.

When we got outside, the ambulance had stopped in front of the building, right in the middle of the street. A bunch of cars tried to get by, but there wasn't enough room. The drivers leaned out the windows, waved their arms, and yelled. But all we could hear were their horns, which they honked and honked without taking a break. Papi had to shout when he told Sarita to go with her sister to the hospital, and said we would take the boys to our house. She hugged him and thanked him over and over. Then she reached over and hugged me too. "Thank you so much!" she said to me with tears in her eyes.

I wondered what Lucy and Sarita would have done if we hadn't come over. What if something really bad had happened? If it had been up to me, we wouldn't have helped them, so I didn't think I deserved that hug. I looked away and said, "Okay, well, good luck. We'll take good care of your brothers." Sarita nodded and hugged me again before climbing into the ambulance.

Sarita's brothers ran like wild people down the street. Papi called them over and grabbed each one by the hand. He tried to chat with them the way grown-ups do sometimes, asking them their ages, if they were excited about becoming uncles, what their favorite subjects were in school. I walked behind them with my sisters.

"What's the matter?" Rosie asked me. "Are you sad?"

I looked at Rosie and thought about her question. Of course I was sad. I had wanted to go see the Eleanor School and find out what I could do to increase my chances of getting a scholarship. And now that wasn't happening. The information session was halfway over by now, and Papi wouldn't want to bring those fidgety boys anyway. My eyes started to water again. But Rosie was just a little kid. She wouldn't understand.

I blinked and shook my head. "No, Sarita and Lucy needed us, and I'm glad we helped them." A part of me just said that so she wouldn't worry. But another part of me really meant it.

Chapter 20

PAPI KEPT HIS PROMISE AND CALLED the Eleanor School on Monday. They said there would be an open house in October, with all the same presentations from Saturday's information session. "You see," Papi said. "I knew it would all work out." I nodded but I didn't say anything. Who knew what would come up on the day of the open house? I would just have to keep my fingers crossed.

Papi came home from work early one day to take Mami to the doctor and get her test results. When my parents got back home, they sat us down and told us the baby was healthy. "Now we have a decision to make," Papi said. He held up an envelope. "The doctor wrote down if the baby is a boy or a girl, and put the paper in here. Do we want to know now, or should we wait until the baby is born? We thought we'd put it up to a vote."

"Now! Now!" Rosie jumped up from the love seat and

raised one hand up high, as if she were trying to get the teacher's attention in school.

"Yes, now!" Connie grabbed Rosie's hands and the two of them jumped up and down.

"Oh, but surprises are so nice," Abuelita said.

"I'm with Abuelita," Gracie said. "I love surprises."

"It looks like you're the tiebreaker, Ana María," Papi said.

Why were they asking us? Why didn't they just make up their own minds? "I don't care. Do whatever you want." I had more important things to worry about, like studying for my scholarship test and learning a super tough piece to play at Lincoln Center.

Gracie frowned at me. "Does that mean you don't want to know now?"

"It means I don't want to make this decision. I mean"—I looked at Mami and Papi—"I don't want you complaining if you don't like what I decide. Remember the bathroom?"

A few years earlier my parents decided the bathroom needed a coat of paint, and they said Gracie and I could pick the color. When we agreed on neon green, my parents nagged us until they talked Gracie into beige. I still wanted the green, but the bathroom had been beige ever since. Why did they bother pretending we had a say in anything?

My parents looked at each other for a while, like they were having a whole conversation without saying a word. Then Papi stood up. "You're absolutely right. Your mother and I should figure this out."

My parents decided not to open the envelope. They put it high up on the china cabinet underneath the super sharp sewing scissors, and ignored it after that. Our trip to the Dominican Republic was three weeks away and Mami was freaking out. "We don't even have suitcases!" she said. So we spent two whole days traipsing from store to store seeking the best deals on luggage. Then we went back to the very first store.

"We've been here already!" Gracie said.

"I know, and now I'm sure this is the best place to buy."

Then Mami announced that we needed new clothes to put inside the suitcases. "We can't bring our old clothes on vacation," she said.

Well, that didn't make any sense. But I didn't argue. Rosie and Connie were thrilled. They hardly ever got new clothes. Mami "shopped" for them in the bins of hand-me-downs in the hall closet.

"We'll go to Chichi's and Lydia's stores next week," Mami said.

And we did. Every day. But we did more than shop for clothes. Twice we brought lunch with us and ate with Chichi and Lydia. We stayed almost the whole day. At least Chichi's brats weren't there, but still, I had things to do. "I need to study and practice piano," I said on the third shopping day. "Can I go home?"

"All by yourself?" Mami said.

"Yes. I walk to Doña Dulce's alone, and that's even farther."

"All right, but call here as soon as you get home, and lock the door behind you."

The first thing I did when I got home was call Mami and let her know I was still alive and well. Then I sat at the piano. I played a little, but I couldn't concentrate. Maybe I wasn't used to all the quiet.

I started thinking about that envelope under the sewing scissors. I should have voted. After all, I did not like surprises. Would it make a difference to my parents if they got a son this time? Maybe. Or maybe not. I would have to think about that. But first I'd have to know what I was dealing with. I mean, if the doctor's note said "girl," then I didn't need to worry about whether having a boy around would change things at home.

I got up and walked over to the china cabinet. I reached up, lifted the scissors, and slid the envelope out. I would take a quick peek. I wouldn't tell my family. They obviously didn't want to know, so why ruin the surprise for everyone else?

The envelope was sealed. I held it up to the light, hoping to see through it. No luck. I could use steam to open the envelope, then I would seal it back with a glue stick. Surely no one would notice. I went into the kitchen and put a pot filled with water on the burner. The telephone rang while I waited for the water to boil. "Hello?"

It was Mami. "I'm sorry to interrupt your studies, but there is an adorable bathing suit I want to get for you. They have them in orange, navy blue, and hot pink. Which color would you like?"

"Um, I don't know, whatever you think is nicest," I said. My heart thumped. I turned my back to the kitchen and stared at my feet. I felt guilty about opening the letter without telling Mami. It felt like a lie.

Mami blathered on and on about shorts and sundresses and different patterns and colors. Finally, finally, she hung up. I let out a long breath and felt my shoulders relax. Then I turned around.

A tall orange flame fluttered next to the pot on the stove.

Chapter 21

I GRABBED THE BURNING ENVELOPE BY THE one safe edge and slammed it into the sink. I turned on the cold water and watched the fire go out. My chest heaved as the white corner and some shriveled dark brown bits of paper swirled in the sink.

I turned to the gurgling stove and shut off the burner. Then I looked up at the china cabinet. Mami would definitely notice something was missing underneath the scissors. I could take a piece of paper from the printer, write either *boy* or *girl* on it, and put it in one of the envelopes from Papi's desk drawer. But which word to write? Maybe there was a clue in the surviving bit of paper, like a *g* or a *y*. I picked up the dripping sliver of envelope and peeled it like a banana, revealing the small scrap of paper inside. I turned the paper over slowly, hoping the back was not blank like the front. But it was. I turned the paper back and forth a few times and wished for a miracle. None came.

It was getting late. Mami and my sisters would be home soon. I opened up all the windows to let out the smoky smell. Then I scooped everything out of the sink, squeezed the water out of the paper fragments, and took the ruined letter out of the apartment and down to the trash room at the end of the hallway. I rushed back and rinsed the pot, dried it, and put it away. Then I put my hands on my hips and looked around. No one would know I had even been in the kitchen. Now I had to work on a new envelope.

I got the envelope and the piece of paper. Now, *boy* or *girl*? I decided to write *girl*. After all, that was probably right. And if it wasn't, so what? If my parents checked the note before the baby was born, and then they had a boy, they would be so happy they wouldn't even worry that the doctor had made a mistake. At least that's what I told myself.

By the time Mami and my sisters got back home, the fake envelope was underneath the scissors, the windows were closed again, and I was practicing piano.

"You're not finished yet?" Mami said.

I had just started. "Um, almost," I said. I was going to tell her that I had studied first and now I needed more time at the piano. But I had lied enough in one day, and I wasn't that good at it, so someone might get suspicious. I got up from the piano and went to my room to work on a practice test.

✳ ✳ ✳

I couldn't stop thinking about that envelope. I told myself that no one would ever figure out what I had done. Even if my parents changed their minds about opening it, there was nothing fishy about what was inside. I had written in all capital letters, so they wouldn't recognize my handwriting. There was absolutely nothing to worry about.

Then why couldn't I stop worrying? Every time Mami had friends over and they talked about the baby, I worried. Whenever she put her hand on her swelling belly and said the baby was moving, I worried. At night after my sisters and I went to bed, I worried. I lay awake, listening to my parents talk in the living room, and I wondered what they were saying. Were they discussing the baby? Would they look now, without the rest of us there? Maybe. Or maybe they would call a family meeting one day so we could all find out together.

I would have asked my friends if they had any suggestions, but Claudia was at field hockey camp now, and every time I saw Ruben, his mother was lurking nearby. Everybody knows grown-ups can't be trusted. So I just worried alone.

One night I woke up in the middle of the night in a panic. What if the doctor had typed the note, and my parents had seen her pull the paper out of the printer? When they saw my handwritten note, they would know something wasn't right. What would I do when they looked at me and said, *What's the meaning of this, young lady?*

I couldn't take it anymore. I put on my glasses, got up, and stood on the ladder to the top bunk. I reached over and lifted Gracie's hair off her face. "Gracie," I whispered. Nothing. I called her again, just a little louder. But not too loud. I couldn't risk waking Rosie. "Gracie," I said one more time. This time I shook her too.

Finally, Gracie opened her eyes and blinked a few times. "What's the matter?" she said. "Is someone sick?"

"No, I just can't sleep." Then I told her everything.

Gracie propped herself up on her elbows. Her eyes popped wide open when I told her about the fire. She even smiled a little, like she was proud of me or something. "Don't worry, Anamay," she said when I finished talking. "Your plan was brilliant. They'll never figure it out."

"But what if the doctor typed the note?"

"Oh, she probably didn't." Gracie lay back down and faced the ceiling. "But I guess she might have." She bit her lower lip. "Okay, this is what we'll do. We won't let them open the envelope. Ever."

"How do we do that?"

"We tell them over and over how much we want it to be a surprise. And you have to join in this time." She poked me in the chest. "Don't act like you don't care again."

"Okay." It wasn't a great plan, but it was better than nothing. And now that Gracie was on my side, this secret seemed so much lighter to carry. I would have to remember this feeling the next time Gracie was upset. Even if I didn't have a solution to her problem, just talking might help her a little.

"Now get some sleep," Gracie said. "Mami's waking us up early tomorrow."

I had forgotten all about the hairdresser appointment in the morning. Mami wanted us to get gussied up for our flight the day after. "Ugh, I hate getting my hair done."

Gracie yawned. "You're so weird. Who doesn't like looking beautiful? Well, anyway, you have no choice. So, good night." She turned onto her stomach and faced the wall.

I climbed back down and crawled under my sheets. For the first time in almost two weeks, I fell asleep right away.

Chapter 22

WE GOT UP SUPER EARLY THE day of our flight to the Dominican Republic. The suitcases were packed and waiting by the door. We just had to fill our backpacks, where we could bring whatever we wanted—supposedly. "No library books," Mami said. "They might get lost or damaged."

If I couldn't bring library books, why bring a backpack at all?

Papi walked in and handed me a white plastic bag. "I picked these up for you on my way home from work yesterday."

I looked inside and saw two books: How Tía Lola Came to ~~Visit~~ Stay by Julia Alvarez, and the seventh Harry Potter book, which was long enough to keep me busy for at least a week! I grabbed the books and held them against my chest. "Thanks, Papi!"

Mami clapped her hands. "Okay, let's hurry up. The airport shuttle will be here any minute!"

I arranged my new books carefully inside my backpack alongside the Chopin and Liszt books, the "Meine Freuden" sheet music, and the books of scales and finger exercises. We put on the new clothes Mami had ironed and laid out for us the night before. I didn't have to do much to my hair. It was still straight from the intense blow-drying at the hairdresser the day before. It looked just like Gracie's. I smiled in the mirror and tossed my head back. Then I followed Mami out the door.

When the elevator got to Abuelita's floor, she wasn't there. "Anamay, go see what's keeping your grandmother," Mami said. "We'll go down and wait in the lobby."

Abuelita had tears in her eyes when she opened her purple door. "I don't know where your uncle is! He should be here by now! What if we miss the flight?"

"Maybe Tío Lalo is already on his way to the airport." Even as I said that, I knew it couldn't be true. But still, we weren't all going to miss our flight because of my flaky uncle. Would I have to argue with Abuelita about this? Luckily, the phone rang.

"Lalo! Where are you?" Abuelita screamed into the phone. "Oh?" She lifted her eyebrows as she listened. Then she smiled and lowered her voice. "Okay, *mijo*. Good, good, I'll see you tomorrow." She put the phone down and picked up her purse. "Lalo traded in his plane ticket for a cheaper flight in the middle of the night," she said. "He saved a lot of money that way. He's so resourceful."

I took Abuelita's suitcase and went to the door. "Didn't Tía Nona buy his plane ticket?" I said.

"Yes."

"So is he giving her the extra money?"

"I don't know." Abuelita locked her door and walked down the hall without looking at me.

When we got downstairs and Abuelita told Mami and Papi about Tío Lalo, my parents just looked at each other and shook their heads.

* * *

The airport was huge and full of people rushing around and bumping into one another. Mami told Gracie to hold on to Rosie and not let go, and I was in charge of Connie. I had the easy job since Connie clung to me until we got on the plane and were buckled into our seats. I felt sorry for Gracie, though. Rosie was so excited she couldn't stand still. Gracie breathed a sigh of relief beside me as she clicked on her seat belt with Mami, Connie, and Abuelita in between her and Rosie.

I got why Rosie was so excited. I was excited too. What would it feel like to be up in the air? To set foot in a different country, a country full of family? Would I be comfortable around these people, or would they feel like strangers?

Connie let out a delighted squeal when the plane lifted off the runway, and all the people sitting near us laughed and said "aww." For the next three and a half hours, Gracie listened to music she had downloaded to her phone, Mami and Abuelita took turns telling Connie stories, Papi read a newspaper, and I started *Tía Lola*. And hyper little Rosie fell sound asleep, looking like a perfect angel.

Chapter 23

THE FIRST THING I NOTICED WHEN we stepped off the plane was the sticky heat. My hair fell down past my shoulders when we left our house, but now it frizzed out and crunched up around my neck. Even Gracie's hair curled up a little, but not like mine. It felt like a furry animal was on my head.

We got our suitcases, and Papi showed our passports to some men in khaki uniforms. They waved us through, and we went back outside where cars and vans were lined up waiting for passengers. A bunch of men ran around and grabbed people's suitcases, then asked where they needed to go. Mami, Papi, and Abuelita kept snatching our bags away from them. "We have family picking us up!" they said over and over again.

Suddenly Mami screamed and opened her arms out wide. A woman who looked like Mami with a tan was screaming too. They ran into each other's arms and clung together, crying and crying.

Finally Mami let go and the woman went through the same routine with Abuelita. Then the woman hugged Papi and said, "It's been too long, *compadre*." Next, she grabbed Gracie's face and cupped it in her hands. "You must be Altagracia! I'm your Tía Chea. I haven't seen my little sister Mecho in sixteen years! And now here she is with her whole beautiful family!" She started to cry again. Suddenly she let go of Gracie and hurled herself at me. I took a step back to keep from falling over under her hug. "Ana María!" She held me in her strong arms. "Rosalba! Consuelo!" She crouched down and hugged my little sisters in one swoop.

"Where's Nona?" Mami asked.

Tía Chea smiled. "She's at her house getting things ready. This is a very special occasion, all of us together again." She laughed and hugged Mami and Abuelita again. "Come on, let's get you home."

Tía Chea and her oldest son, Pepito, who was seventeen, had brought a van so there would be room for all of us. We piled in and rode for a long time. I started to count the palm trees along the road, but there were too many. And the bright sun made my eyes water, so I closed them, just for a second.

"Anamay, we're at Tía Nona's house." Gracie shook my arm to wake me. I looked out the van window. We were in front of a white two-story house with a wraparound porch and a wavy red roof. The white rocking chairs on the porch had colorful pillows on them: red, orange, yellow, green, and blue. When we slid the van doors open, the smell of burning

128

charcoal and meat reminded me of summer barbecues at Claudia's house.

The place was packed with people. A stereo perched on a sideways-leaning table on the front lawn. It was attached to a thick orange extension cord that snaked into the house. The speakers on either side of the stereo jumped with each beat of merengue music. As we got out of the van, the crying and hugging started all over again.

Papi introduced us to his two brothers, three cousins, and four nephews from the nearby village where he was born. Papi's oldest brother, Tío Rogelio, was wearing a Yankees cap and a T-shirt that said "Columbia University." He put an arm around Papi and squeezed him. "My baby brother," he said. "A big-shot New York lawyer! Who would have thought?"

"All of us," his middle brother, Tío Marcos, said. He stood on Papi's other side and patted him on the back. "This guy," he said to me, "was the smartest kid for miles. When the teacher was sick, he was the substitute. Even for the older kids!" He and Tío Rogelio laughed. Papi blushed.

"It's true," Tío Rogelio said. He pointed at me. "This one must have your brains," he said to Papi. "I can see it in those eyes."

"Ana María is a very good student."

"You see? I knew it! I can tell these things!"

"Ana María, has your father told you about our baseball games when we were kids?" Tío Marcos said.

I shook my head.

"We were unbeatable!" Tío Rogelio said. "You remember that, don't you, Tavito?"

"Of course," Papi said. "You pitched, I caught, and Marcos ran like the devil getting away from church!" The three brothers howled and slapped each other's backs.

"We were a great team," Tío Marcos said.

I met a lot of people that day. Juan Miguel introduced us to his parents and a bunch of his cousins and aunts and uncles. We met Tía Chea's husband, Tío Pepe, and his father, Don Feyo, who lived with them. We also met Tía Chea's two younger children, Juancito, who was fifteen, and Muñeca, who was thirteen like Gracie. Then there were a bunch of old people—Abuelita's cousins and friends, and even an aunt of hers. The aunt sat in a rocking chair the whole time. When I walked up to say hello, she grabbed my hand and wouldn't let go. "So you're the pianist," she said. "We're all so proud of you!"

How did all these people know so much about me? It felt a little weird, but also kind of nice, like I belonged with them.

* * *

It was dusk when Mami pulled Gracie and me aside. "Would the two of you like to stay at Chea's house?"

"Oh, yes, yes, yes!" Gracie said. She had hung out with Muñeca all afternoon.

I looked around. We were in one of Tía Nona's living

rooms, which was bigger than our one and only living room at home. It had a gigantic couch with carved wooden legs that curled under it, two matching chairs with fluffy pillows, three fancy lamps with golden fringe dripping from their edges, and a sparkling white baby grand piano. Mami had told us this room was just for decoration. There was a whole upstairs too. "Why? Isn't there enough room for all of us here?" I said. If we could all fit in our apartment, surely we could squeeze in here.

Mami leaned forward and whispered to us. "Chea will be offended if nobody stays with her. And I think the two of you could handle it."

"That's fine," Gracie said. "We'll go."

"What do you mean, 'handle it'? What's wrong with Tía Chea's house?" I asked.

"Well, nothing. It's just that she's a little old-fashioned." She looked at me, then at Gracie, then back at me again. "Her water situation isn't what you're used to."

"What does that mean?" I said.

"Well, there aren't toilets and sinks inside the house."

What?! "How long do we have to stay there?"

"Oh, it'll be fun, Anamay," Gracie said. "Like camping, right?"

Mami stared into my eyes and held her hands together like she was praying or something. "Okay," I said, even though I didn't want to.

Suddenly, the room got dark and the music stopped.

We heard groans outside. "Not again!" someone said.

Gracie grabbed my arm. "What's going on?"

"It's just a blackout," Mami said. "That happens a lot here."

Outside, an engine purred, then roared. The lights flickered until they were back on, and I jumped when the music started up again. "What is that noise?" Gracie asked.

"It's the generator," Mami said. "It kicks on whenever the lights go out."

"Does Tía Chea have a generator?" I asked.

"Probably not."

Great.

* * *

Gracie and I climbed into the van with Tía Chea and her family. It wasn't far, but the electricity was still out, so the roads were super dark. When we arrived at their house, Tío Pepe used a flashlight to guide us to the front door, and Tía Chea lit two oil lamps inside. Muñeca gave us a tour.

"You'll sleep in here with me," she said, lifting the curtain that blocked the doorway between the bedroom and the living room. Inside were two beds with mosquito nets hanging over them. A bare cot sat in one corner. "I don't need a net," Muñeca said. "But you *americanas* will be eaten alive without one."

The outhouse was behind the house, but not too close—maybe a city block back. Muñeca led the way, flashlight in hand. We were still a few feet away when the stench hit me. It sort of reminded me of the stairway to the subway, but way worse. Muñeca reached for the metal handle on the door of the windowless wooden hut. "Make sure you don't touch the door," she said. "You could get splinters." She pulled the door toward her and walked right in. She didn't hold her breath or pinch her nose with her fingers or anything. Once inside, she pointed the flashlight at a metal string hanging from the low ceiling next to a lightbulb. "When the lights are working, you pull on that," she said. "But always bring a flashlight with you, just in case." Then she pointed the light down at the only thing in the room: a wooden bench with a hole in it. A roll of toilet paper sat beside the hole. "If you need to go in the middle of the night, the flashlight will be on the night table in our room."

I made a mental note not to have anything more to eat or drink that evening.

Tía Chea, Tío Pepe, and Don Feyo were talking in the kitchen when we got ready for bed. Moths and beetles circled the small oil lamp on the table, sometimes almost landing on their cheese and crackers, or in the tiny cups of black coffee they were drinking. No one seemed to mind. They just kept chatting, and casually waved a hand at the pests every few minutes.

Muñeca handed each of us a glass of water, and got one for herself. "Let's brush our teeth," she said.

We went outside and brushed our teeth in the quiet

darkness, spitting water onto the dirt. I looked up at the sky, and was amazed by the way the stars completely filled it. You can't see stars in New York City. Here, there were millions. And everything was so quiet. Maybe Gracie had been right about this being fun. Or at least different. Maybe I could write about this for one of the essays required on the scholarship application. That would probably help me stand out from the other kids.

Then I felt an itch on my knee, and one on my ankle. Soon I was scratching everywhere and slapping the buzzing mosquitoes away from my ears. I ran back in the house and under the safety of the mosquito net.

Chapter 24

THE NOISY CRICKETS MADE IT HARD to sleep. Their eerie chirps were nothing like the soothing sounds of car horns and sirens at home. And just when I finally dozed off, the roosters started to crow.

I was exhausted in the morning, but I couldn't sleep anymore. Outside, people were laughing and calling out to each other, and dogs were barking away. I lifted the mosquito net and slipped out of bed and into my flip-flops. I took two steps toward the doorway, then stopped to look at Gracie and Muñeca, who were still sound asleep. I slowed down my steps and tried to tiptoe, but the suck-slap-suck-slap of my shoes still seemed super loud.

When I got to the living room, I looked around. Tía Chea's house reminded me of Abuelita's apartment. The framed painting of the *Virgen de Altagracia* by the front door and the family photos all over the orange walls were exactly like the painting and photos on Abuelita's orange walls. And

Tía Chea's doors were purple too! The back one was ajar, so I peeked outside. Tía Chea was walking out of the little wooden building behind the house—the kitchen, Muñeca had told us the night before.

"*Buenos días*, Anamay!" Tía Chea held a pan of still sizzling sausage in one hand and a plate with crispy *tostones* in the other. I held the door open as she came inside. "Go wake up the girls, and I'll get the boys." She put the plates on the table. "We have a lot to do today."

Those were the best *tostones* I had ever eaten. Tía Chea said it was because the plantains were freshly cut that morning. Maybe staying on a farm wasn't such a bad idea after all, as long as I hid out under the mosquito net at night.

After breakfast, Tía Chea clapped her hands. "Pepito and Juancito, get the water for the baths! Muñeca, bring towels and washcloths for your cousins, then make the beds! And you two"—she pointed at Gracie and me—"get your clothes and don't take too long in your baths."

My clothes and towels were bunched up in my arms when Pepito walked in with a giant bucket of water from the tank outside. I followed him into the bathroom, which was small and square and had a very low wall that ran down the middle of the room. When Pepito set the bucket down on the other side of the wall, I realized that side was the bathtub. "That should be enough water for three people," he said before he walked out and closed the door behind him.

I rolled my hair up into a bun before stepping into the

bathtub. I didn't need a shower cap since I was just pouring cupfuls of water from the bucket on myself. The first scoop of cold water over my shoulder made me jump and squeal a little. After a while I sort of got used to it. And it felt nice to lather Tía Chea's perfumed soap on my sticky, sweaty skin. But still, I couldn't stop thinking that my parents and little sisters were probably taking nice warm showers at Tía Nona's house.

"Anamay, hurry up!" Gracie pounded on the door. "The rest of us have to bathe too."

I reached into the bucket for another scoop. That's when I noticed I had used more than half the water. I watched the soapy water slide outdoors through the hole in the corner of the bathtub. Was anyone standing out there? Could they see that I was hogging all the water?

"I'm sorry," I said when I got out of the bathroom. "I think I used too much water."

"Oh, don't worry about it," Tía Chea said. "Juancito, go get some more water!"

Juancito ran outside. He didn't seem to mind lugging another huge bucket of water to the house. But still, I would have to figure out this whole water thing if I was going to stay here a while. And it looked like I was.

* * *

Tío Pepe and the boys stayed to work on the farm, and Tía Chea took Muñeca, Gracie, and me to Tía Nona's. "We have to put the party favors together," Tía Chea said. "The more hands, the better. The wedding is less than a week away and we're expecting a lot of guests."

Mami, Abuelita, and Tía Nona were already working when we got there. Glue bottles, stickers, and little white bows were scattered on a picnic table underneath a shady tree that stretched above the house. A stack of boxes sat next to the table. "Oh, I'm so glad you're here!" Tía Nona gave us long hugs. "Would you like some lemonade?"

"Absolutely," Tía Chea said. "It's going to be a hot one today." She took off her sun hat and fanned herself with it.

Tía Nona turned to the door. "Cosita!" she called. "Cosita, come here!"

A skinny girl just a little taller than Rosie ran out of the house. Her bare feet were caked in dried mud and there were tiny holes all over the front of her sleeveless shirt. "*Diga, doctora*," she said to Tía Nona.

"Bring out a pitcher of lemonade and some glasses."

"*Si, doctora*." Cosita ran back in the house.

Gracie and I looked at each other, then huddled close to Muñeca. "That little girl *works* here?" Gracie whispered.

"Yeah," Muñeca said.

"Isn't that kind of weird?" Gracie said. "I mean, she's just a kid."

Muñeca shrugged. "Some kids from really poor families have to work."

"Okay, girls," Tía Nona said. "Come see what we're

doing." She reached inside one of the boxes and took out a tiny champagne bottle. "We take these out, grab a label"—she picked up a sheet of heart-shaped labels that said "María Antonia y Juan Miguel" and peeled one off—"and we stick it on the bottle." She took her time and put the label on the very center of the bottle. "Then we take one of the bows and glue it on the neck of the bottle." The bows had the wedding date printed in gold letters. Tía Nona squeezed a pearl of glue onto the middle of the bow and held it tightly against the bottle. She looked back up at us. "Okay?"

We all nodded.

"Oh my goodness, I'm so hot!" Tía Nona said. "Where is that girl? Cosita! Cosita!"

Cosita came out with a giant pitcher of lemonade.

"Oh, *mamita*, let me help you with that!" Mami said. She took the pitcher from Cosita.

"Where are the glasses?" Tía Nona glared at the girl.

"I'll get them right now, *doctora*."

Mami put the pitcher on the table. "This looks delicious," she said.

"The glasses, Cosita!" Tía Nona yelled.

Cosita ran out the door with a stack of three glasses in each arm. She tripped and fell to her knees, but she held on to the glasses. Gracie and Muñeca ran over and helped her up.

"Well, at least you didn't break anything this time." Tía Nona snatched the glasses from Cosita and put them on the table. Then she turned back and looked at the blood trickling from the girl's knobby knees. "Let's clean you up before you get an infection." She grabbed Cosita's hand and yanked her up the steps and into the house.

"What's gotten into Nona?" Abuelita said when Tía Nona was inside. "She's being so cruel to that little girl."

Tía Chea lowered her voice and leaned in close to Abuelita. "It's that Juan Miguel," she said. "He's very sweet to Nona, but he and his family are terrible to their servants. I think it's rubbing off on Nona."

Abuelita shook her head. "I'm going to have a talk with her."

"Oh, Mamá, don't make any trouble," Mami said. "Nona's probably stressed because of the wedding."

"Well, that's no excuse," Abuelita said.

"I agree with Mamá," Tía Chea said. "Nona's letting those people take over and change her. Can you believe the reception is at their house?"

Muñeca covered her face with her hands. "Oh no, not this again."

"Well, it's an insult!" Tía Chea said. "Nona has a family, and the bride's family should host the wedding reception!"

"Calm down, Chea," Mami said. "Nona explained the whole thing to me. Juan Miguel's mother wanted the wedding at one of their hotels, but Nona said she had to be married in the church where she was baptized. And she got her way."

"Yes, but why is the reception at their country house?"

Sweat dripped down Tía Chea's neck and onto her flowered T-shirt. "My house is just as close!"

"It's too late to change that now," Abuelita said. "But she can't treat the help like that."

"Who can't treat the help like what?"

We all jumped. Where had Tía Nona come from? She glared at Abuelita. "Are you talking about me?"

"Of course we are! I'm ashamed of you, Nona! I didn't raise you to mistreat people, and you have been very rude to that poor little girl!"

Tía Nona walked over to the boxes of champagne bottles. "You have no idea what that girl has put me through, Mamá." She took out a bottle and reached for the labels. "She's broken half my things, she steals food, and the other day Juan Miguel's mother and I were waiting for her to bring our coffee and she never came. I found her lying on my good couch sound asleep!" Tía Nona looked at Abuelita. "I've kept her on because I know her family needs the money, but I'm beginning to lose my patience. And I can't believe my own family would talk about me behind my back!"

"Oh, Nona," Mami said. "We're sorry." She put her arms around Tía Nona. "We shouldn't have judged you. Right, Mamá?"

Abuelita crossed her arms and nodded like she didn't really mean it. "Well, okay, fine," she said. "We're here to help, so let's get to work."

Gracie, Muñeca, and I looked at one another. I wasn't

sure whose side to take. I mean, maybe everything Tía Nona said about Cosita was true, and it seemed unfair for Abuelita and Tía Chea to gang up on her. But still, Cosita was just a kid, and she seemed to be doing the best she could. She didn't deserve to be yelled at like that. But Tía Nona wouldn't be unfair, would she?

"Hey, Tía Nona, I never knew your first name was María," Gracie said as she pulled a bottle out of a box. That Gracie was pretty good at changing subjects.

Tía Nona smiled. "We're all named María," she said. "Chea is María Dorotea, and your mother is María Mercedes."

"That's right," Abuelita said. "María is a blessed name, and I wanted all my girls to have it." She looked at me. "I was so happy when your parents named you Ana María. Traditions are very important."

"Speaking of names," Tía Nona said, "do you have names picked out for the new baby, Mecho?"

Mami stuck a label on one of the bottles and rubbed her fingers over it again and again. "We haven't come up with a girl's name yet, but definitely Gustavo Junior for a boy," she said.

"But what would you call him?" Tía Chea asked. "We already have one Tavito."

"He doesn't need a nickname," Mami said. "We can just call him Gustavo."

"Or his nickname could have nothing to do with his actual name, like mine," Muñeca said.

"Why is your nickname Muñeca anyway?" I asked.

Tía Chea reached across the table for a bow and chuckled. "The boys came up with that. They thought their baby sister looked like a doll. Before we knew it, we were all calling her that."

"I like my nickname," Muñeca said. "It makes me feel beautiful and special."

We all laughed. Not too many people would like being called a doll, but as long as she was happy . . . I thought about what Abuelita had said about my name, and I held my head up high too.

Chapter 25

WE HAD FINISHED LABELING ABOUT HALF of the bottles when Cosita came out and told us lunch was ready. We went into the dining room and sat at a long table under a crystal chandelier. The cook brought out platters of roasted chicken, rice, pinto beans, salad, and fried ripe plantains. Every time she came into the room, she yelled at Cosita to get out of her way. "You're going to make me drop this food, you useless girl!" So Cosita planted herself in a corner of the room and did not move.

The white walls in the dining room were covered with framed paintings and wooden artifacts. "Where are those from?" I asked Tía Nona.

She looked at the masks I was eyeing. "Oh, different places. Some are African, and some Asian. And this"—she tilted her head toward a painting on the other side of the room—"is our latest acquisition from our trip to Spain. It's an El Greco print. Isn't it beautiful?"

I nodded as I looked at the spooky landscape in the painting.

"Isn't there anything Dominican in here?" Abuelita asked.

Tía Nona laughed. "Oh, Mamá," she said.

"I'm starved," Mami said. "And everything smells delicious."

We passed the food around and served ourselves heaping platefuls. "When does Lalo get here?" Tía Chea asked.

Tía Nona snorted. "He called this morning. Apparently, he missed his flight last night."

"Don't worry, Nona, he'll be here in time for the wedding," Abuelita said.

"Oh, I'm not worried. Either he'll make it or he won't. Whatever."

Abuelita's face got all tight and pinchy. "Well, you do need him to walk you down the aisle."

Tía Nona put her fork down. "About that, Mamá. I really want you to walk with me."

"What? That's unheard of! It has to be the man of the family!"

"No, it doesn't. It should be the parent, and you're my only parent now, so I want it to be you." Tía Nona reached over and put her hand over Abuelita's. "Please. It would mean so much to me."

Abuelita patted Tía Nona's hand. "Well, okay, if it's important to you. But only if Lalo doesn't mind. I don't want to offend him."

"Don't worry, I'll talk to him."

We ate until we were stuffed. Still, there was a lot of food left over. Abuelita looked over at the corner where Cosita was standing. I had forgotten she was there. "Are you hungry, *mamita*?" Abuelita asked.

Cosita glanced at Tía Nona. She shook her head and looked down at her feet.

"She'll eat in the kitchen when we're done," Tía Nona said. She turned to the girl. "You can take these plates now and bring the ice cream."

Cosita sprang toward us and grabbed the half empty chicken platter. When she came back from the kitchen, the cook was right behind her. "Take the silverware and saucers," the cook said to her. "I don't want you to drop any of these heavy platters."

"Tía Nona," I said when Cosita was in the kitchen. "Is that her real name?"

"Who?"

"Cosita." I couldn't imagine anybody naming their child "little thing."

Tía Nona laughed. "No, I just call her that because I can never remember her name. Besides, she probably won't last long here, so why should I bother?"

Well, that seemed kind of mean. But maybe Tía Nona figured the girl would leave at the end of the summer. After all, she did have to go to school, right? And my aunt already had so many names to remember, with all her patients.

Cosita and the cook came in with the ice cream and bowls. Then Cosita took her place in the corner again.

"Come here, *mamita*," Abuelita said to her. When Cosita stood beside Abuelita, my grandmother put her hand on the girl's arm. "What's your name?"

Cosita looked down at her feet and spoke softly. "Clarisa."

"Oh, okay," Tía Nona said. "I was close." She dug her spoon into her ice cream and took a mouthful.

"How old are you, Clarisa?" Mami asked.

"Eleven."

"My Anamay is eleven too!" Mami pointed at me by puckering her lips in my direction.

Clarisa kept her gaze on the ground.

"What grade are you in?" Abuelita said.

Clarisa lifted her head and stared at Abuelita. "Grade?"

"Yes, at school."

Clarisa looked at Tía Nona.

"Why don't you go in the kitchen and have your lunch now, Cosita," Tía Nona said.

Clarisa smiled and ran off.

"Doesn't she go to school?" Mami said.

Tía Nona shrugged. "Probably. I don't know any kids her age that don't."

"Well, shouldn't you find out to be sure?" Abuelita said.

"Why? That's not my problem."

Mami's eyes opened wide, but she didn't say anything.

"Nona," Abuelita said, "that little girl looks up to you and depends on you. As her employer, you have to treat her well and help her better herself."

"She's not my child." Tía Nona licked the ice cream off her spoon. "She came to me for a job, and I did her the favor of giving her one. As far as I'm concerned, I've done more than enough."

Abuelita opened her mouth. Before she could say anything, Mami touched her arm and shook her head just a little. My grandmother pursed her lips shut and picked up her spoon. She scooped some half-melted ice cream and slurped it like soup.

Abuelita reminded me of Papi when he talked about the needy people in our community and how we should all help one another. And Tía Nona was like me. I always told Papi that other people's problems weren't my responsibility. We should all take care of ourselves. But Clarisa was just a little girl, and maybe her family couldn't help her. But Tía Nona could. If she wanted to. Obviously, she didn't want to, and no one could make her.

Chapter 26

AFTER LUNCH I WENT TO THE living room to practice piano while the rest of the family watched television in the recreation room. Tía Nona had asked me to play Bach's Prelude in C Major for her entrance into the church, and the music was already on the piano. I warmed up with scales and finger exercises. Then I decided to play something fun. Something Claudia would sing when we hung out together, except there wouldn't be any singing this time. But that was okay. I could imagine her voice in my head, singing John Lennon's "Imagine." It started softly. And it seemed so real, like she was standing right next to me.

I stopped playing and turned around. "Clarisa! I didn't know you spoke English."

Clarisa shook her head and clutched the feather duster in her hand. "I don't speak English."

"But you know that song."

Clarisa shrugged. "I've heard it on the radio, but I don't know what it means."

"Should I keep playing while you sing?"

Clarisa nodded fast, a big smile on her face. I started again. Her voice was beautiful, even better than Claudia's. And I couldn't believe she didn't know what she was saying. "Do you want me to tell you what the words mean?" I asked after we were done.

Clarisa nodded and sat next to me on the piano bench. I went through the song line by line and translated it for her. "That's beautiful," she said.

"You have a great voice," I said. "Do you sing in a choir?"

She shook her head and jumped up. "I have to finish cleaning in here."

"I'm sorry," I said. "Did I upset you?"

Clarisa smiled. "I'm not upset. I just have to clean or your aunt will be mad. But you keep playing. Listening to you makes the work go faster."

I was happy to hear that. At least I was helping a little. "Do you know this one?" I started to play Adele's "Someone Like You," and Clarisa immediately joined in. She moved around the room dusting and singing. A couple times she stood still, held her arms in front of her, closed her eyes, and sang her heart out. She seemed to be having so much fun that I played the song a second time.

In the middle of a note, Clarisa suddenly stopped singing. I figured she was just taking a breath, but she remained silent. Then I looked up and saw Tía Nona standing in the doorway.

"That's very nice, Anamay," she said as she walked in and stood by me. "How is my wedding song coming along?"

I looked at Clarisa. She was dusting away, not looking at us. "I was just about to work on that," I said. "I was warming up first."

Tía Nona smiled. "Of course." She moved away. "I don't want to interrupt the artist at work! Come, Cosita, this room is fine. Go clean up the kitchen now."

I wanted to tell my aunt about Clarisa's wonderful voice. After all, that was the kind of thing we would normally share. And Tía Nona always appreciated true talent. But somehow, it didn't seem like the right thing to do. So I just watched her leave the room, with Clarisa trotting behind her. Then I practiced Prelude in C Major, one hand at a time, again and again.

After about an hour, I went outside to join my family on the porch, where we rocked in the rocking chairs like old ladies. Tía Nona handed me a wicker basket covered with a cloth napkin. "Here you go, Anamay," she said. "We saved some *turrón* for you."

"What's *turrón*?" I said as I took the basket and peeled back the napkin.

"Oh, you're going to love it," Tía Nona said. "It's made from coconut. And, of course, lots of sugar."

I lifted a thick tan square out of the basket and took a

bite. I opened my eyes wide as I crunched on the most delicious thing I had ever eaten in my life. "This is sooo good!" I said. There were two more pieces in the basket, and I ate them both.

Tía Nona laughed. "I knew you'd love it, because I do too!"

After I finished every last crumb, I was truly stuffed. I sat back and rocked some more. I was about to doze off when a dusty pickup truck crunched into the pebbled driveway. Tío Rogelio honked and waved at us from the cab. Papi and my little sisters got out of the truck, and Tío Rogelio pulled away. Rosie and Connie ran over and grabbed my hands. They pulled me down the steps and onto the front yard. "Anamay, listen to this game our cousins taught us."

"Which cousins?" I said.

"Rogelio's boys," Papi said. He sat in my chair.

Muñeca and Gracie came down to join Rosie, Connie, and me. "What game?" Muñeca said.

"I don't know the name of it," Rosie said. "Just watch." She and Connie faced each other and clapped their hands while they sang about a skeleton guarding a cemetery. Each hour of the day, the skeleton ate or drank something.

De la una a las dos, el esqueleto come arroz

They put their hands to their mouths and pretended to eat rice just like the skeleton. While they "ate," they sang some more.

Chumba que chumba que chumba ba

Then they clapped again.

De las dos a las tres el esqueleto bebe café

They held pretend cups and sipped their coffee like the skeleton.

Chumba que chumba que chumba ba

This went on until they got to the eight to nine o'clock hour.

De las ocho a las nueve el esqueleto no se mueve.

Now the skeleton stood still for an hour, and Rosie and Connie competed to see who would move first.

Muñeca laughed and clapped her hands. "I love this game," she said. "I used to play it all the time when I was little."

We watched Rosie and Connie and waited for someone to budge. But they were too good. Finally, Gracie got tired of looking at them.

"Let's play, Muñeca," she said. Gracie kept messing up the words. She was supposed to say, *De las siete a las ocho el esqueleto come sancocho*, but instead of having the skeleton eat stew, she gave him cake. Rosie doubled over in laughter.

"Not *bizcocho!*" she said. *"Sancocho!"*

"Ha ha. I win! I win! I win!" Connie ran around with her arms up like a victorious boxer.

The sun was beginning to set when we got into Tía Chea's van. I looked back at Tía Nona's house as we pulled away. Clarisa came out of the front door with a large paper bag in each hand. She turned in the opposite direction from us and walked into the blinding dusk with her head down and her shoulders slumped. She looked so tiny, like a little sister who needed someone to take care of her. I had had fun hanging out with her that afternoon. It seemed unfair that she had to work while I just loafed around for hours. What would her life be like if she lived in New York and we sat next to each other in school? We would probably be friends. Could we be friends now?

Chapter 27

THE NEXT DAY WE BROUGHT OVERNIGHT bags to Tía Nona's because she had promised to take us someplace fun. "We can finish the champagne bottles later this week," she said. "You girls need to see the beach!"

The whole family piled into Tía Chea's van. Well, there was only room for twelve of us, so Tío Pepe said he would follow in the pickup truck with Pepito and Juancito. "You don't both have to squeeze into the truck," Tía Chea said to the boys. "There's a spot here beside your grandfather." Don Feyo patted the seat next to him, but my cousins insisted the truck was more fun.

"Tía Nona, what's Clarisa doing today?" I asked.

Tía Nona squinted at me. "Who?"

"The girl that works for you." I was not going to call her Cosita.

"Oh, Cosita? She's got laundry to do. Why? Do you need something?"

"No, I just thought that, since we have room for one more, maybe she could take the day off and come to the beach with us."

Tía Nona laughed and shook her head. "It's not a good idea to fraternize with the help." She looked over at her house. "Although it might be helpful to have her around to carry things for us."

"Carry things? But she's so little!" Did my aunt think Clarisa was a mule or something?

"You need your laundry done, Nona," Mami said. "Come on, let's go."

It took almost two hours to get to Puerto Plata. Connie asked about every flower and tree she saw along the way. Papi tried to answer her questions, since Mami—the real tree and flower expert—was engrossed in wedding talk with Abuelita and my aunts. Gracie and Muñeca giggled about cute boys, and Don Feyo showed Rosie some card tricks.

I couldn't believe everyone was acting so normal. Didn't it bother my parents that Tía Nona would treat a child like she wasn't even a person? Maybe she was still mad at Clarisa for breaking her stuff. That would make me mad too, if it really happened.

Juan Miguel and his parents were waiting for us at their hotel when we pulled up. The place was amazing, with palm trees stretching out of wooden boxes throughout the lobby, shiny marble floors, and fountains that looked like water-falls. Muñeca's mouth dropped open when we walked into

156

our room. "This is so luxurious!" she said. She ran around stroking the lace curtains, the ginormous television, and the leather love seat in the sitting area. Then she plopped herself down, grabbed the remote, and clicked through every channel in the universe.

Gracie admired the embroidery on the linen bedspreads, then went to see the bathroom. Rosie was already in there. "Look at me!" she said as she tripped in a way-too-big-on-her fluffy white bathrobe.

"That's for after you shower, silly!" Gracie helped Rosie out of the robe, and went to hang it back up.

"Let's check out the balcony," Rosie said. I stepped outside with her and felt the warm ocean breeze against my face. The beach was right there. Cool.

"Hi, Anamay!" Connie was in the neighboring balcony, where she was staying with my parents.

"Get your swimsuits on, girls," Mami said. "We should take advantage of this beautiful beach."

It really was beautiful. I put a toe in the water expecting to feel cold, but it was as warm as a bath. Then I walked all the way in up to my shoulders. When I looked down, I could see clear to my feet. This had to be the cleanest beach in the world!

"Anamay, I want to introduce you to some friends!" Tía Nona was at the water's edge in an orange two-piece. A bunch of glamorous people were with her. She introduced me as her brilliant niece who was so much like her. The friends all bragged about themselves. One woman had been Tía Nona's classmate and was now the top oncologist in the country. At least that's what she said. One man was a top businessman, another one the best lawyer, and the other woman had perfect children who were nowhere to be seen.

Abuelita came over and draped a giant towel over Tía Nona. "A respectable girl like you should wear something more modest," she said.

Tía Nona rolled her eyes. "This is my mother," she said to her friends as she took off the towel and handed it back to Abuelita. "I don't need this."

Mami kept slathering sunscreen on my little sisters and telling Gracie and me to put some on too. I did at first, but then I had too much fun in the water to bother reapplying it. When we went back inside, my shoulders were bright red and what should have been a wonderful shower was very painful. I should have listened to my mother.

The day ended with a lobster dinner at a fancy restaurant in the hotel. Our family sat at two tables—one for the grown-ups and one for the kids. Pepito and Juancito cracked us up doing impressions of all the snooty people we met that day, but they made sure to speak softly so Tía Nona and Juan Miguel and his family wouldn't notice.

I felt a little guilty about making fun of my aunt's friends. We wouldn't even be here having such a great time if it weren't for her and her fiancé's family. So I couldn't decide if I should join my cousins and sisters in the fun, or if I should scold them and stick up for Tía Nona's friends. I ended up enjoying my cousins' impressions. After all, maybe those people were just acquaintances and my aunt was only being polite to them. And she was nothing like them, right?

When we finished eating, I watched the waitresses and busboys running around with sweat on their foreheads, hauling huge trays of dishes. I wondered if Clarisa would ever get to enjoy a place like this.

✳ ✳ ✳

We spent most of the next day at the beach again, and piled into the van to head back in the early evening. "I need to go to the clinic tomorrow," Tía Nona said, looking at her phone. "Some patients are asking about me, and I have to complete some paperwork before I go off on my honeymoon."

"Do you want us to finish the champagne bottles?" Mami asked.

"No, there aren't that many more to do," Tía Nona said. "We can finish them on Friday. Just enjoy yourselves tomorrow."

So Tía Chea dropped Gracie, Muñeca, and me off at Tía Nona's house the next day, then went back to help Tío Pepe and the boys on the farm. "Don't get too used to this," she told her daughter. "When your cousins go home to the United States, it's back to work for you, young lady."

"I know, I know." Muñeca grabbed Gracie's hand, and the two of them started to run off.

"Where are you two going?" Tía Chea called.

"To socialize with the neighbors!" My sister and cousin kept moving. I had heard Muñeca tell Gracie that some cute fourteen-year-old twin boys lived near Tía Nona.

Tía Chea probably knew about those boys, because she shook her head and shouted for all the world to hear, "You come back here if their parents aren't home!"

After Tía Chea left, my parents, my little sisters, and Abuelita sat on the porch and entertained a stream of visitors. Everyone acted like we were celebrities or something. "You're the one who hasn't been back in sixteen years!" a bunch of people said to Mami. I went inside to practice piano. The wedding was two days away and I had to perfect Prelude in C Major. It wasn't too tough, but everyone would be watching and I would be nervous.

Clarisa came in while I was practicing. "That sounds good," she said after I had played it twice.

"Thanks. Do you want me to play something for you to sing?"

Clarisa smiled and reached into the front pocket of her shorts. "Do you know this song?" She handed me a wrinkled sheet of paper.

I took it from her. It was an old merengue by the Dominican singer Johnny Ventura. "I've never played this before," I said. "But I've heard it." At Gracie's graduation party, actually. Could I play this like Sarita did?

"This is my favorite song," Clarisa said. She sang a few

lines and danced along without waiting for me to join her on the piano. "Guess what?" she said suddenly. "I'm moving to Santo Domingo with my mother."

"Really? When?"

Clarisa looked at her hands. "I'm not sure. Whenever she makes enough money to get a place big enough for the whole family."

"Where does she work?"

"She sings at a nightclub and she's really good. Right now she just gets food, a free room, and fancy dresses to wear on stage, but her boss says that when the club starts to make more money, they'll pay her. And he said I can work with her when I'm thirteen."

"Wow. No wonder you're so good. It's in your blood."

Clarisa blushed. "I can't wait until I'm thirteen."

"What about school?" I said.

"I don't need school anymore," Clarisa said.

"Oh," I said, "are you allowed to drop out of school at your age?"

Clarisa shrugged. "My parents don't make me go anymore. There's no time for that. But . . . could you show me how you know which notes to play?" She sat down next to me at the piano.

In less than an hour, Clarisa was reading music. Well, all the notes around middle C at least, which was really impressive. She was so smart. It was a shame that she didn't want to keep going to school.

"I'm going to miss you when you go back to the United States," Clarisa said.

"I'll miss you too. Maybe I can teach you to play a song, and then we'll think of each other when we play it."

"I'm not allowed to touch this piano. I'm only playing now because you're here."

"Oh." I wondered if I should say something to my aunt about that. Would she give Clarisa permission to practice for a little while each day? I wanted to believe that she would, but I had to admit that I didn't really think so. "Maybe you can get your own instrument, something small to play at home—"

"Cosita! Cosita!" The cook was calling her.

Clarisa jumped up. "I'll see you later!" she said with a big smile on her face.

I wondered how Clarisa could be so cheerful when she had so little. I got whiny just because my parents didn't want to pay for the Eleanor School. Would anything ever upset Clarisa?

Chapter 28

THE DAY BEFORE Tía Nona's WEDDING, we went back to her house and finished decorating the champagne bottles. After lunch, everyone sat on the porch and talked. I couldn't stop thinking about Clarisa, though. She was probably cleaning up the lunch dishes all by herself. It didn't seem fair. She was just a kid. Did she ever get to play or relax?

"I'm going inside to practice piano," I said.

"Oh, good," Tía Nona said. "We want my wedding song to be perfect." She gave me a wink and a smile.

I walked through the dining room and into the kitchen. Clarisa was leaning into the sink, her back to the kitchen doorway. I walked over and saw that she was scrubbing a giant pot. Soap suds had climbed up to her elbows.

"Hi," I said.

Clarisa dropped the pot with a clang. "Oh, hi. Can I get you something?"

"No," I said. "I was just wondering if you need any help."

"Did your aunt send you?"

"No, she doesn't know I'm here."

Clarisa closed her eyes for a second and let out a long breath. "Oh, good. Well, no, I can do this myself." She turned back to the sink and picked up the soapy pot.

"But I want to help," I said. "I wash dishes at home all the time. It's faster when there are two of us." I picked up a dish towel. "Here, I'll dry."

"No! Go away! You'll get me in trouble."

"What are you talking about? You can't get in trouble because of me." I lifted a wet frying pan out of the drying rack.

Clarisa jammed the sponge into the pot, splashing soapy water out of the sink and onto her chest. She breathed heavily and her nostrils flared as she started scrubbing again.

I didn't care if she was too proud to admit she could use some help. I was going to stay and dry those dishes. "When we finish, we can go play music and sing some more," I said. "Trust me, you'll thank me later."

"No, we can't do that today," Clarisa said. "Not with your aunt here."

There was a scratching sound at the kitchen door. "What's that?" I asked.

"Nothing. Just ignore it."

What was Clarisa's problem? She was acting so weird. I put the towel down and went to the door. I opened it a crack and saw a man with a boy about Connie's size. Other

164

than a dusty pair of sneakers, the boy was completely naked. *Completely*. The man wore a tattered hat and a stained short-sleeved shirt over faded plaid pants. He had a stump where his left hand should be, and he held the little boy's hand in his right hand.

I opened the door the whole way. "Hello," I said. "Can I help you?"

The man looked at me with big eyes. "I'm sorry, *señorita*," he said. "We didn't mean to trouble anyone."

"But who are you?" I said.

"That's my father, and he was just leaving." Clarisa stood next to me. "Papá, I told you not to bother me at work."

"But your brother hasn't eaten since yesterday," he said.

"Well, that's too bad," Clarisa said. "You know the rules here. I can't take any food until it's time to go home. Do you want to get me fired?"

"No, no, of course not. But I just thought that—for your brother—he's been sick and—"

"Go away!" Clarisa slammed the door and stomped back to the sink.

I opened the door again. Clarisa's father and brother were walking away slowly. The boy stumbled. I could see his ribs, even from where I was standing. "Wait!" I called out. Clarisa's father stopped and turned around. "I'll get you some food," I said.

"God bless you, *señorita*." They ran back to the kitchen door.

"Okay, wait here." I turned to Clarisa. "Does my aunt have any paper plates?"

"We can't do this," Clarisa said. "I'll lose my job."

"No you won't." I opened some cabinets until I found the paper plates. I took one and dished out some rice, black beans, codfish, avocado slices—a little of everything we had just eaten for lunch. I grabbed a spoon and went outside to hand the plate to Clarisa's brother.

The boy sat down right there on the ground and dug in. "He's been coughing a lot," his father explained as we watched him eat. "It's not good to go all day without eating if you're coming down with something."

I nodded, although it seemed to me no one should go all day without eating, even if you weren't coming down with something. "Would you like a plate too, *señor*?"

"Oh, no, I can wait until Clarisa comes home."

"What's going on here?" Tía Nona walked up behind Clarisa's father and glared at him. "How many times have I told you to stop bothering my family and friends? Cosita! Cosita! Come here!"

Clarisa appeared in an instant, her soapy hands dripping beside her.

"Take off the apron and leave!" Tía Nona said. "This is the last straw! I have warned you over and over about this!"

"No!" I said. I stood in front of Clarisa to shield her from my aunt. "It's not her fault! I offered him food! I brought it to him! He didn't bother anybody! And she didn't do anything wrong!"

"Oh, sweetie, you didn't know any better." Tía Nona put her hand on my shoulder and gave me a light squeeze. "But we can't let these people take advantage of us like that." She turned back to Clarisa and her voice became harsh again. "What are you waiting for, Cosita? Take your family and go!"

Clarisa's eyes hardened on me. "You got me fired!" she said through her clenched jaw. Then she ran off, her father and her brother at her heels.

Clarisa was right. This was all my fault.

"Why did you do that?" I asked Tía Nona. She looked blurry through my tears.

"Rules are rules." She didn't look upset at all, as if she hadn't just ruined a whole family's life.

"But they're hungry, and there's so much food here! How can you treat anyone like that?"

Tía Nona smiled and tilted her head like she was talking to a dumb little baby. "You don't know how to deal with these kinds of people, Anamay. That Cosita was nothing but trouble."

"Stop calling her Cosita! Her name is Clarisa! How would you like it if everyone called you Brujita because you're a mean old witch?!"

Tía Nona's mouth dropped open. I turned and ran.

Chapter 29

I WIPED THE TEARS FROM MY FACE as I ran away from Tía Nona's house. I had to get as far away from my horrible aunt as possible. I remembered from the van ride that, to get back to Tía Chea's house, I had to go past the old pump well that Mami had used when she was a little girl, then go right at the turquoise building with the word "COLMADO" painted in fire-engine red above the outside counter. Then I'd find my way to Tía Chea's house and then . . . then what?

The afternoon sun was super bright and hot. By the time I reached the well, I was sweating and out of breath. I stopped running and decided to walk the rest of the way. I jumped when I heard a car horn. It was Tía Chea in her van. She stopped and Mami got out of the van. "Ana María Reyes, get in here right now!"

Mami stood beside the open van door. I looked at her for a few seconds, wondering if I had any other choice. I decided I didn't.

When we had both climbed inside, Mami turned to me and frowned. "Anamay, what has gotten into you?"

I looked at my lap and shrugged.

"You have to go back and apologize to your aunt."

I lifted my head and faced Mami. "But she was wrong!" I turned away and watched a yellow-and-green house across the road. Two eyes stared at me through a window made of horizontal wooden slats. When I looked back at them, the shutters slammed shut.

Mami took my hands in hers. "Anamay, look at me." I obeyed. "You were right to stick up for that little girl, but you were wrong to be rude and disrespectful to your aunt. Nona's not perfect, but she's family and she loves you."

"She most certainly is not perfect," Tía Chea said. "But I put up with her anyway."

"We all put up with each other," Mami said. "That's one of the great things about family. Nobody's perfect, but we still love and support one another."

I looked at Mami's hands. They were warm and strong and I knew she wouldn't let go until I was ready. Tía Nona didn't deserve an apology, but I could see this was important to Mami. And maybe I could convince my aunt to give Clarisa her job back. After all, maybe Tía Nona just didn't understand what had happened. Once I explained it to her, she would surely do the right thing.

* * *

Abuelita and Tía Nona were sitting in the chairs on the porch, but they stopped rocking when we got out of the van. Gracie and Muñeca watched from the front steps. Abuelita stood up. "Chea and Mecho, come inside and help me clean up the kitchen," she said.

"You too, girls," Mami said to Gracie and Muñeca. They got up and followed the grown-ups without argument.

I stood in front of Tía Nona. She was wearing a big diamond-studded pendant on a chain around her neck, and I kept my eyes on that. "I'm sorry for speaking to you so rudely, Tía Nona. It was wrong of me and I hope you will forgive me." I sounded like a robot, but I didn't care.

"Oh, of course I forgive you!" Tía Nona wrapped me in her arms. She let go and held me by the shoulders. "But am I really a mean old witch?" She had a big smile on her face.

I forced myself to smile a little. "No. I was just mad, and I couldn't think of anything else to say. But I didn't mean it, honest I didn't."

"Oh, I know." Tía Nona hugged me again.

Now was my chance. "But you know . . . Clarisa didn't do anything wrong. She told me not to open the door for her father, but I did it anyway. Then she told me not to give him any food, and I didn't listen to her. You should be mad at me, not her."

Tía Nona gave me that poor-dumb-baby look again. "Oh, Anamay, I know you feel responsible, but believe me, you're not. This is Cosita's father's fault for coming here in the first place. He's the one who wants her to work, so he has to follow the rules."

"But what if they starve to death? Won't you feel guilty?"

"*Ay, mamita*, you worry too much. They'll be fine." Tía Nona put her arm around my shoulder and led me toward the door. "Let's not think about anything unpleasant today. Tomorrow is the most important day of my life! Let's focus on that, okay?"

"Can't you give her one more chance? Please?"

Tía Nona put her hands on her hips and shook her head. "I've given Cosita too many chances already. Now, please, let's get back to important things." She turned and walked into the house. The door swung shut behind her.

I stood there and looked at the closed door. Tía Nona seemed different from the person I always thought I knew—a person who cared about other people and treated them fairly. How could I have been so wrong about her? And now that I knew the real Tía Nona, could things ever be the same again? I put my head down and walked into the house slowly.

My family was in the kitchen, cleaning up and talking wedding stuff. I thought about Clarisa as I put away some dishes. Under that holey shirt, did her ribs stick out like her little brother's? When would they eat again?

"I need to practice piano," I said.

"Oh sure, go ahead!" Tía Nona shooed me away with a smile.

I couldn't concentrate on Prelude in C Major, so I put my hands on the piano and let them play "Für Elise" without giving it much thought. I was thinking about Clarisa instead. It wasn't fair that she was only eleven and she had to work to feed her family. That was too much responsibility for a kid. What could I do to help her? Maybe if I talked to her, she would tell me. Or would she be too mad? Would she forget that we were friends and just see my aunt's niece when she looked at me—the girl who got her fired? My fingers pressed on the piano's firm, hardly used keys, and the sounds were clear, crisp, sweet, and sad at the same time.

I opened my eyes when I finished playing. Soft clapping began behind me, which got louder and louder. I turned around and saw Mami, Abuelita, my aunts, and Gracie and Muñeca standing in the doorway to the living room. "Bravo!" Tía Nona said.

"That was beautiful, *mamita*," Mami said.

Abuelita wiped her eyes, and Tía Chea, Gracie, and Muñeca nodded as they continued to clap.

I wasn't sure what I had done to deserve this. Was this what Doña Dulce meant when she told me to play from the heart? If it was, then I didn't like it. My heart hurt with sadness.

Chapter 30

THE WEDDING WAS AT THE CATHOLIC church in the nearby town of Salcedo. Pepito took the van to Tía Nona's house to pick up the rest of my family while Gracie, Muñeca, Juancito, and I rode in the back of Tío Pepe's pickup truck. We girls had to hold down our matching yellow skirts in the wind, and the road was so bumpy our butts hurt by the time we got there.

The church was loud with chatter and laughter. Mami and Tía Chea led Muñeca and my sisters to the front pew. Papi, Tío Pepe, and the boys sat behind them. I took my sheet music to the front of the church and sat at the piano. There were a lot of familiar faces there, but I couldn't remember many names. It was so hot I could hardly breathe. My sweaty dress clung to me, and beads of moisture rolled down my arm like they would on a glass of ice water on a summer day. Three long candles on the altar drooped to the side.

I looked at the music in front of me and hoped I didn't mess anything up. I listened to the hum of a hundred voices talking at the same time and the rustle of paper as people fanned themselves with prayer books and wedding programs and whatever else they could find. Finally, the organist played a few notes to quiet everybody down. Juan Miguel stood by the altar dripping with sweat. Then the priest looked at me and nodded. I started to play Prelude in C Major. Tía Nona entered the church with a beaming Abuelita by her side. My grandmother seemed to be okay with walking Tía Nona down the aisle after all.

Tía Nona came down the aisle and joined Juan Miguel at the front. I finished the Prelude without any mistakes, and when the priest started to speak, I snuck over to sit with my family. Mami cried as Tía Nona and Juan Miguel read the marriage vows they had written themselves. They talked about making each other better people and blah, blah, blah. Tía Chea probably didn't agree with that. After all, she said Juan Miguel and his family were making Tía Nona a snob. Maybe I agreed with her. Or maybe Tía Nona had been a snob all along. After the way she treated Clarisa, I was sure my aunt was not becoming a better person, Juan Miguel or no Juan Miguel.

Finally Tía Nona and Juan Miguel kissed, and then everybody clapped and cheered. The priest told us to go in peace, and the organ played while the happy couple walked toward the door. I peeled myself off my seat and followed my family outside. We stood in a line outside the church and hugged a bunch of sticky people. A few of them asked Abuelita the same question: "Where is your son?"

Abuelita waved her arm each time, and said, "Oh, he's around here somewhere."

But he wasn't. Tío Lalo never showed up.

* * *

We got back in the pickup truck to go to the reception at Juan Miguel's parents' country house. The party was outside, with food served on tables under a bunch of white tents. The band played a Juan Luis Guerra song while Tía Nona and Juan Miguel danced. Then the band's singer announced that it was time for the bride to dance with her father and the groom with his mother. "Unfortunately," he said, "the bride's father is watching us from up above, so her older brother will dance with her in their father's place."

Tía Nona had said she didn't care if Tío Lalo never showed up, but now she was looking all around for him, and her eyes were getting shiny. Mami nudged Papi with her elbow, and he walked over to my aunt and held out his hand. She smiled and took it. Abuelita cried as we watched Papi and Tía Nona, and Juan Miguel and his mother, on the dance floor. I couldn't tell if she was sad that Tío Lalo wasn't there, or happy that Papi had saved the day.

When the rest of the guests were invited to join in, my whole family stepped forward. Gracie and Muñeca danced with those twin neighbor boys, my parents twirled Rosie and Connie around, and Pepito led Abuelita onto the dance floor. Juancito asked if I wanted to dance, but I didn't feel like it. Especially not when I heard the Johnny Ventura song that Clarisa had said was her favorite. I watched kids take glasses of lemonade from the servers, only to spill half of them right away, and I saw chunks of cheese and nibbled-on empanadas all mashed up on the ground. How much food and drink was being wasted at this one party? How many people were going to bed hungry tonight just a few miles away? I served myself a small plate and sat at a table feeling guilty as I nibbled at my meal and looked around. When I saw Tía Nona laughing away, I got kind of mad. How dare she be so happy after what she had done to Clarisa! She had no right.

* * *

After Tía Nona left for her honeymoon, my whole family stayed at Tía Chea's house. I shared my bed with Connie, and Rosie slept with Gracie.

"This is so much fun," Muñeca said when we were all tucked into bed. She pointed her flashlight to the ceiling. She had promised to keep it on until Connie fell asleep. "It's like a slumber party. You guys are so lucky to have each other. I wish I had sisters."

"I wonder if Clarisa has any sisters," I said.

"Who's Clarisa?" Rosie asked.

"Tía Nona's maid. Well, she's not her maid anymore since Tía Nona fired her."

"Hmm, I think she has a sister," Muñeca said. "I've seen a little girl running around outside her house, but I guess she could be a neighbor or a cousin."

"Wait!" I sat up in bed. "You know where Clarisa lives?"

"Yeah, she's not too far."

"Can you take me there tomorrow?"

"Oh, it's not close enough to walk," Muñeca said. "But my dad could drive you."

"Would he do that?"

"Sure, why not? We'll ask him in the morning."

✳ ✳ ✳

Tío Pepe said he would be happy to take me to see Clarisa. Muñeca and my sisters wanted to come too, but my parents said no. "We don't want Clarisa and her family to think you're going over to gawk at them like they're animals at the zoo," Papi said.

So it was just me and Tío Pepe in the pickup truck. "What will you say to her?" he asked.

I opened my mouth, then closed it again. I realized I had no idea what I would say. "Well, I guess I'll apologize for making her lose her job."

"That's a good start." Tío Pepe made a sharp right turn onto a narrow dirt road. There were no street signs anywhere.

"Also, Papi told me to give her this." I showed him the crumpled twenty-dollar bill in my hand.

"That's even better."

Tío Pepe swerved to avoid a cat licking her kittens in the middle of the road. He made another turn and slowed down to a crawl when we got to an area with houses crowded together on both sides of the road. This was so different from Tía Nona's neighborhood, where the houses were huge and far apart, and from where Tía Chea lived, with smaller, neat and colorful houses surrounded by fruit trees. Some houses here had thatched roofs, and others had rusty metal ones. Wet towels, shirts, and socks hung on bushes and clotheslines and in the gaps between the wooden slats of the house frames. Toothless women laughed and shouted out to one another from yard to yard. The muscles on their wiry arms flexed as they wrung out clothes, holding them at arm's length until the water dripping from the cloth slowed to a trickle. Diapered toddlers ran between the women's scarred legs, shrieking with laughter as they chased one another. Everyone stopped what they were doing to stare at us when we pulled up in front of a faded blue house. "This is it," Tío Pepe said.

I got out and took a deep breath, trying to slow the thumping of my heart. I hoped this visit would actually help, but I wasn't sure that it would. I followed the sound of voices coming from behind the house and found the naked boy tossing a dirty tennis ball to a little girl in a ripped-up dress.

"Hi," I said.

The boy waved at me. He whispered in the girl's ear, and she waved too. Then she ran inside and immediately came back out dragging her father by the hand.

"*Señorita!*" Clarisa's father said. "Welcome, welcome. Please, come inside."

"Oh, no, that's okay," I said. "My uncle's waiting for me in the truck, but my dad told me to give you this." I wanted to ask to see Clarisa, but I wasn't sure if I should. Maybe she was busy. Or still mad. I remembered how she had looked at me when I got her fired, and I didn't want to see that look again.

Clarisa's father took the twenty-dollar bill. "God bless you. Thank you, thank you."

Clarisa came out of the house carrying a bucket of wet clothes.

"Clarisa! Look at this!" Her father held up the bill.

Clarisa looked at me with cold eyes. "We don't need your charity," she said. "My family and I work for everything we have."

"But you earned this," I said. "It's your last pay from my aunt."

Clarisa knew I was lying. Her father surely knew that too. She looked at her family one by one. They smiled at her, showing their small brown teeth. She did not smile back. Finally, she turned to me. "Thank you for bringing the money." She walked to the clothesline.

"Okay, well, goodbye," I said.

"Goodbye, *señorita*, and thank you." Clarisa's father took the two little ones and went back inside.

I looked at Clarisa. "Do you need any help with the laundry?"

"No!"

I kicked a pebble back and forth from one foot to the other. "Look," I said. "I'm really sorry about what happened the other day. I had no idea my aunt would fire you. I was just trying to help."

Clarisa kept her eyes on her work. "Yes, of course. You rich people never have any idea about anything."

I gasped. "I'm not rich!"

Clarisa reached into her bucket and plucked out a shirt. "Oh really? Have you ever gone to bed hungry?"

I paused, but I didn't need to think about my answer. "No."

"Do you have shoes?"

I looked at her bare feet. My voice was soft when I spoke. "Yes."

Clarisa turned to me with her hands on her hips. "You think you know everything, but you don't! When my family needed me to work, everyone said I was too small and useless, but your aunt gave me a chance. Then you came and ruined it!"

She reached down and grabbed another shirt, then another one. She jammed the clothespins fiercely into the

180

laundry on the wire. The lines leaned toward the ground, then bounced back up, over and over again.

I tried to think of something to say. Nothing came to mind. I walked back to the truck and told Tío Pepe I was ready to leave.

Chapter 31

WE STILL HAD A FEW MORE days left in the Dominican Republic, and we spent all of them visiting relatives. Tía Chea was happy to drive us around and hang out drinking a *cafecito* at each house. Mami wouldn't have any because she said the caffeine wasn't good for the baby. There was a lot of talk about the baby. Everybody had a theory about whether it was a boy or a girl. Tío Rogelio's wife said it was definitely a boy and that she was never wrong. But Tío Marcos reminded her that she was wrong about his last child, and that started a whole argument that ended in laughter and more *cafecitos*—except for Mami, of course, who had lemonade like us kids.

My cousins—I think they were all cousins—were pretty nice, but not that interesting. Rosie and Connie had fun running around and playing stickball with the younger boys, while Gracie and Muñeca got makeup tips from the older girls. I was glad to go to Tía Nona's house each day and practice piano. I even decided on my recital piece: "Meine Freuden" by Chopin and Liszt like Doña Dulce had suggested. It was super tough, and I would have to practice a lot after we got back home, but I thought I could handle it if I worked hard. And it would definitely impress Eleanor's head of school—I hoped.

Whenever I thought about going to Eleanor, I got excited. But then I'd think of Clarisa, working all day in her bare feet, struggling to make sure her family had enough to eat, and I'd feel kind of silly. How could I think about new textbooks and Latin classes when kids like Clarisa were going to bed hungry every night? But what could I do to help those kids? I didn't have any idea, so I just concentrated on my music. At least that was something I could control.

* * *

There was a lot of crying and hugging at the airport the day we left the Dominican Republic, just like on the day we arrived. But the tears were not happy this time. And the adults weren't the only ones crying now. Gracie and Muñeca vowed to write to each other every day, and Connie and Rosie begged my parents to let us stay longer.

I wished we could stay longer too. I had finally gotten the knack of using just the right amount of bath water, and the sunburn I got the first week didn't hurt anymore. Plus, Tía Nona wasn't back from her honeymoon yet. I was sure I could get her to hire Clarisa again if I only had a chance to talk to her one more time. Now that the wedding was behind her and she was relaxed, she would surely see that she had overreacted. I would have loved to tell Clarisa she had her job back. But I was out of time.

"Don't wait another sixteen years before you return," Tía Chea said to Mami. "I want to meet my new niece or nephew soon." She rubbed Mami's belly and sniffled.

"We'll be back." Mami put her arms around Tía Chea's neck, and the two of them cried and cried.

"Come on, Mecho," Papi said. "We don't want to miss our flight."

Mami let go of Tía Chea and took a step back. Abuelita was sobbing on Pepito's shoulder. She looked up and threw herself at Tía Chea. The two of them clung to each other like suction cups on glass. Papi looked at his watch, and Mami saw that. "Mamá, come on," she said. "The plane might leave us."

Tía Chea peeled herself off of Abuelita, then turned to say goodbye to the rest of us. When it was my turn, I felt her warm tears drip onto my neck. "Take good care of your mother and your sisters," she said. To Gracie she said, "Be good."

When we were on the plane, I looked over at Mami and saw that she was still crying. What would it be like to go sixteen years without seeing one of my sisters? Even though they sometimes got on my nerves, I couldn't imagine being apart from them for more than a few days. My parents lived so far from most of their relatives. How could they stand it? Maybe this was why they treated everyone in our neighborhood like family. A substitute family is better than no family at all.

Chapter 32

AFTER WE GOT HOME, IT WAS like we had never left. Papi went to work every day. Mami cooked, cleaned, and did laundry. Gracie sewed with Mami and hung out with her friends. Rosie helped Mami cook and talked about the start of her new year of ballet classes in September. Connie got her hands dirty helping Mami with the plants. And I practiced piano and worked on my scholarship application by myself. On Sundays after church Ruben and I made flash cards with questions that might be on the scholarship exam.

"Thanks for helping me," I said to him, "especially since you don't even want me to go to that school."

Ruben grinned. "This will help both of us with the Science test too—just in case you decide you don't like Eleanor."

"True," I said. I couldn't imagine not liking Eleanor, but I could imagine not getting a scholarship, and I had to prepare for that possibility. So Ruben and I made more flash cards each week.

Soon it was time to get ready for school. Gracie grumped about being required to wear a uniform to Little Bethlehem, and about the fact that all her friends got to stay in public school for high school. I thought about Clarisa when we shopped for school supplies and for new first-day-of-school outfits for Rosie and me. How well did she know how to read and write? Wasn't it against the law for her to stay home from school?

Claudia came over for a sleepover at my house. I had told her everything. "If Tía Nona won't help Clarisa, then I will," I said.

"Really? How?"

"I'll raise money and send it to her."

"Can I help?"

We thought and thought about how to make some money. "We could go door to door and tell people about Clarisa," Claudia said. "Or we could set up a GoFundMe page."

"I don't know," I said. "My parents would never let me go to people's houses begging for money. And GoFundMe seems too much like begging for money too."

"At my school—well, *our* school next year—we sell stuff sometimes, like gift wrap, to raise money," Claudia said.

"Yeah, we could sell stuff!" I said. "But what? We'll have to make something."

We decided to sell cookies and lemonade outside Claudia's house. "That's a wonderful idea!" Mami said. She and Rosie made a huge batch of Mami's famous honey almond cookies.

Claudia and I made chocolate chip. Gracie painted a sign for our stand. Connie helped her color in the letters.

The next morning Claudia's mom drove us to her house, and we made a giant pitcher of lemonade. As soon as we set up the stand, a kid on a bike came by. When he tasted one of Mami's cookies, he ran off to get more money and to tell his friends. In no time, we sold $128 worth of lemonade and cookies. I called Tía Nona when I got back home.

"Anamay, *mi amor*! It's so good to hear your voice. Your mother tells me you've been busy with the piano."

"Yeah, the recital is in December, and 'Meine Freuden' is really challenging," I said. "There are a few tricky parts I need to work on, and then I have to memorize it, but at least there's plenty of time."

"I'm sure you'll be fabulous. We're all so proud of you. And now I can finally tell you about my honeymoon!" Then Tía Nona blabbed on and on about snorkeling and visiting the beautiful waterfalls and national parks in Fiji. "Oh, and the food was just divine!" she said.

I only halfway listened to her. Usually, I would be super interested in my aunt's adventures, but I had something else on my mind. When she finally stopped talking, I took in a deep breath. "Um, I was wondering, do you have Clarisa's address?"

"Who's Clarisa?"

She knew who Clarisa was. "The girl you fired when I was at your house."

"Oh, her. Why do you ask?" Tía Nona's voice got all uptight and annoyed.

"Well, it's just that we've been getting ready for school, so that got me thinking about her and wondering if she's getting ready for school too. So I raised some money and I want to send it to her."

"Oh . . . well, that's very nice of you."

"Do you know where I can send it?"

"Yes, yes, hold on a second."

While Tía Nona went to get Clarisa's address, I wondered if I should ask my aunt to give Clarisa her job back. The thing was, I didn't really think Clarisa should be working at all. But if she didn't work, how would her family survive? The $128 would help a little, but then what?

"Tía Nona," I said after she read the address to me, "do you think you could maybe help Clarisa's father find a job?"

"*Ay*, Anamay, I can't take care of every poor child in the world! I'm just one person!"

"I know, but can't you help one child? And Clarisa isn't just a random kid. She worked for you." I wished I could reach into Tía Nona's brain and make her agree with me.

"Put your mother on the phone, please. I want to see how she's doing."

"Okay," I said. That didn't go very well. At least I got Clarisa's address. Maybe I could think of something more to do for her later. But cookies and lemonade couldn't help forever.

The weekend before school started, my family went to the furniture store. "To take advantage of the Labor Day sales," Papi said. We were getting another bunk bed in our room, and Connie would move in. I had known for a while that this day was coming soon, and Connie already spent a lot of time in our room anyway. But I worried about this fifth kid. There was definitely no space for one more bed in our little room.

Rosie was super excited. "I get to sleep on top! I get to sleep on top!" She did cartwheels all over the store and almost knocked over a lamp on display.

"Calm down," Mami said to her. "Anamay, are you sure you don't want to move over to the new top bunk?"

"I'm sure," I said. "I like things the way they are. Where would I put my glasses up there?"

Mami shook her head. "All right." She turned to Rosie. "No jumping on your new bed, and no somersaults either."

"I know, I know," Rosie said. But did she really know? I hoped so.

"One somersault and Mami will make us change beds," I said to Rosie. "She won't take any chances with safety. You know that."

"I said I know." Rosie put her hands on her hips. "Stop treating me like a baby!"

"Well, stop acting like one."

"You're so bossy!" Rosie turned her back on me, but she didn't do any more cartwheels in the store. I hoped I had gotten through to her.

Chapter 33

THE FIRST DAY OF SCHOOL WAS exciting for me, as always. Would I like my teachers? What new things were out there waiting to be learned? I got up at the same time as Gracie, even though she had to leave earlier to take the subway to her new school. It felt weird to walk to school without her. At least I had Ruben. "Are you sad that this might be your last year in this school?" he asked as we walked into homeroom.

I shrugged. "I guess, a little." But then I got a splinter when I leaned on my desk, and I saw that three pages had been ripped out of my math textbook, so I thought: *No, I'm not sad at all.*

It was the second week of school when Mami handed me an envelope that came in the mail for me. "It's from Nona," she said.

Gracie looked over my shoulder as I unsealed the envelope.

"A picture? Why did she send you a picture?"

I examined the photograph. It was Clarisa and her dad. Clarisa wore a bright white shirt and navy-blue pants. On her feet were black-and-white saddle shoes. Shoes. Clarisa was wearing shoes.

I looked inside the envelope for a note. Nothing.

"There's something written on the back," Gracie said.

I turned the photo over and saw a handwritten note:

Dear Anamay,

Here is a photo of my new gardener and his daughter on her first day of school. He asked me to thank you; with the money you sent, they bought her school clothes, shoes, and supplies.

Love,
Tía Nona

"Look, Mami, we did it!" I said. "We helped Clarisa and we convinced Tía Nona to help her too."

Mami squeezed my shoulders and kissed my forehead. "No, *you* did it, *mamita*. And I'm very proud of you."

I was pretty proud of me too. When Papi got home from work, I showed him the photo and note from Tía Nona. "I'm so happy I helped Clarisa," I said to him. "Is this how you feel at work every day?"

Papi laughed. "I wish I could say yes, but unfortunately,

I'm not always successful at helping my clients, even though I try my best. When I am, though, it does feel great."

"Maybe I should check out your job on Take Your Children to Work Day."

"That would be wonderful, Ana María!"

I skipped to my room to study for the Eleanor scholarship test. Take Your Children to Work Day wasn't until the spring, but I was already looking forward to it.

$$* * *$$

The big sale at Cristina's Fabrics was on the first Saturday in October. Mami wanted to get there super early to make sure the material and supplies for my recital dress were in stock. So she and Gracie took all my measurements the night before and wrote down everything we needed. When the three of us got to Cristina's, we elbowed our way in and grabbed all the items on our list: glitter satin for the skirt, lace for the top, and anti-static lining, all in tango red. We also needed matching thread, something called interfacing, and a long zipper. Mami and Gracie had long conversations about the quality and feel of every piece of material in the store, like I wasn't even there. But at least I got to pick the color.

Gracie and Mami planned to start cutting out the pieces as soon as we got back home, but Papi had some bad news for us. "Chichi just called," he said. "Her babysitter quit. She just showed up at the store with the twins and said she couldn't take it anymore."

"Oh no! And on the store's busiest day!" Mami shook her head. "Could you go to the store and pick them up? The girls and I will twin-proof the house before you get back."

I could not believe this. "I really need to practice," I said.

"Okay, then, do it quick while we move some things around."

Mami didn't understand that practicing piano couldn't be rushed. There was no way I could concentrate with Chichi's terrible twins around. So I didn't get my hour of practice that day. Again.

* * *

The next day Mami and Gracie cleared off the dining room table and took out the pattern.

"We're making view B, right?" Gracie said to Mami.

"Yes. So which pieces do we need?"

Gracie unfolded the sewing directions and laid them out on the table. I watched her back as she hunched over and examined the instructions. "We need pieces one, two, four, and six," she said. She and Mami shuffled around, rustling papers and discussing which ones to use and which ones to put aside.

Then Mami called me over to measure the skirt length. I stood still while Mami and Gracie talked about me like I was a mannequin. "Should she put on a pair of your heels?" Gracie asked.

"No, she's too young to wear heels," Mami said. "We'll just add an inch for her shoes."

"An inch? That's not enough! She'll look ridiculous in a too-short fancy gown!"

Finally they agreed that I should put on my church shoes. Mami held the pattern up to just the right spot on my waist, and Gracie got down on her knees with the tape measure. "We only need to take it up three inches," Gracie said.

Mami frowned. "Are you sure?" Mami was probably thinking the same thing I was: that Gracie was sneakily making my dress a little longer so Mami would have to let me wear heels after it was finished.

"Yes, I'm sure!" Gracie's nostrils flared a little. "We need to leave room for the hem, right?"

Mami bent over and looked. "Hmm, okay, that seems right."

I didn't want to wear high heels. How would I walk up to the stage in wobbly shoes? And would that mess up my pedal work? But before I could protest, they sent me away.

✳ ✳ ✳

Every day that month they worked on my dress after Gracie got home from school. But only for a little while each day. Gracie had homework and Mami had to make dinner—with Rosie "helping," dinner seemed to take Mami a long time to finish. So Mami and Gracie cut out the dress a little bit at a time before they started to put everything together in tiny increments.

The dress was kind of like my recital piece—coming along slowly. Except I knew the dress would get finished before the day of the Winter Showcase. I wasn't so sure about "Meine Freuden." Every time I played it for Doña Dulce, I expected her to beam with pride, but she just scrunched up her nose and said, "Almost there. Keep working on it." First she said the tempo wasn't quite right in a few places, so I went home and practiced with the metronome for a million hours. That did the trick—mostly. "Slow down gradually for the ritardando sections," she said. I tried to remember that as I played, but it was hard to get out of the exact rhythm once I had it down. I thought about how I had played "Für Elise" at Tía Nona's house, and how everyone had clapped. Maybe I should always play when I'm sad. But how do you make yourself sad on purpose? Would I ever be able to play like Sarita?

Chapter 34

THE SECOND SATURDAY IN OCTOBER WAS the open house at the Eleanor School. It was for anyone who wanted to learn about the school, not just for scholarship applicants. Miraculously, my whole family was able to make it. When we arrived, we walked through an iron gate that said "THE ELEANOR SCHOOL" on it, and went straight ahead into the main building, which was surrounded by the most grass I had ever seen in New York City.

"Wow," Rosie said, "this looks like a castle!"

My parents laughed. "Maybe we should live here then. We are the Reyes, after all!" Mami said.

There was a long table in the entryway with a sign-in sheet and a bunch of smiling teenagers. "Welcome to the Eleanor School," one girl said. "Here's a map of the campus and a schedule of today's events."

I thanked the girl and studied the agenda. "We need to be in the auditorium in ten minutes for the main presentation,"

I said to my family as I ushered them back outside. Mami held on to Papi and Gracie as she wobbled down the wide stone steps of the main building. Her belly had gotten huge lately and she huffed like a jogger the whole way down.

"Are you okay?" Gracie asked her.

"Yes, I'm fine," Mami said. She put her hand on her back and let out a little groan.

"The auditorium is right over there," I said as I looked at the map. "You'll be able to sit when we're inside."

Rosie and Connie skipped ahead on the brick walkway toward the white building at the end of the path. "This place looks like a college campus," Papi said.

The auditorium was huge. Mami sat down right away. She looked super tired. "Do you want to stay here when we go on the tour?" I asked her as we waited for the presentation to begin.

Mami sighed. "Oh, yes, that would probably be best," she said. "That way I won't slow you down."

Soon the lights flickered and the presenters began. The head of school showed a PowerPoint with information about AP classes, national test scores, and college acceptances. Students spoke about extracurricular activities and field trips to cool places like Washington, DC, and even Europe! The admissions director explained the application process and tuition payment plans. During the tour of the campus, we saw the spacious computer room, the library with floor-to-ceiling bookshelves, and the two music rooms. We learned about the poetry workshop, the journalism project, and the robotics club. When they mentioned the debate team, I saw Papi nod and smile. I felt like I was in a dream. This school was absolutely perfect for me. I couldn't imagine going anywhere else.

✳ ✳ ✳

The scholarship exam was the following Saturday, in the middle of October. I was super nervous that morning. "You have to eat breakfast," Mami said. "You can't take a three-hour test on an empty stomach." But I didn't think I could keep anything down, so we compromised on a glass of orange juice.

Papi rode the subway and then the bus with me to the Eleanor School. We walked up the stone steps to the main building and into the wood-paneled office to check in and submit my completed application. Papi gave me a hug and wished me luck. I went into the room with the sign that said "Grade 8, M–Z" on it and found a seat. All the kids around me looked nervous too. I smiled at the girl sitting next to me, but she didn't seem to notice. She was muttering math problems to herself.

When the test started, I stopped being nervous. The math questions were challenging and fun, and the essay prompts got me to think through and write about some interesting topics. When I finished the last essay, I looked at the grandfather clock in the corner and saw that I had ten minutes to spare. I looked over my answers, but I didn't change anything.

"I think I did well," I said to Papi when I found him waiting for me outside.

"I'm sure you did," he said.

Then I started to wonder. "What if they were all trick questions, and I actually got everything wrong?" I said.

Papi laughed at that. "I'm quite certain you did not get *every* answer wrong," he said. He was probably right. But still, I went home and practiced "Meine Freuden." That was the next step in my journey toward a full scholarship, and I didn't want to blow it.

* * *

At the end of October, one week before my birthday on November 1, Mami took me aside and said we needed to talk. My mind went straight to the envelope under the sewing scissors. Mami and Gracie had worked on my dress a lot lately. Every time they reached for the scissors, the envelope was right there. Maybe Mami took out the note. But Gracie had promised to stop her, and she would have told me if Mami had even mentioned opening the envelope.

Mami went into her room and sat on the bed. "Come sit next to me," she said.

"Is something wrong?" I sat down, but not too close.

Mami looked at her hands. "You know the baby is due in December, right?"

"Yes."

"On Christmas Day."

"Uh-huh."

"Now, babies aren't always born on their due dates. In fact, most of the time they're not. They could be early."

"Why are you telling me this?" I said.

Mami put a hand on my shoulder and looked me in the eyes. "I didn't mention this before because it probably won't happen and I don't want you to worry. But I should warn you that if the baby is born early, there is a very small chance that your father and I may not be able to go to your concert."

"Oh," I said.

"There is also a—again, small—possibility that only I would not be able to make it. If, for example, the baby is born the day before." She ran her hand down my arm and gave me a little squeeze. "Your father will probably be there. He would only miss it if I'm in labor at the time of the recital. And, like I said, that probably won't happen."

"Okay." I got up and walked out of the room. This was so typical. Mami did so many things with my sisters, but she couldn't even come watch me play at Lincoln Center. And Papi too? That dumb baby would probably be born on the day of the Winter Showcase just to spite me. Just to keep my parents away from me. And that would be only the beginning.

* * *

I was mad at my parents after that. I tried to tell myself that it didn't make sense to be angry. After all, my parents had no control over when this baby came. But still, why were they even having another baby when they didn't have time for the kids they already had? They hadn't even mentioned my birthday, even though it was just a few days away. Had they forgotten it? Probably. They probably would forget all my birthdays from now on.

That whole week I avoided everyone in my family. I did what I was told, but nothing more. I came home from school, practiced piano, did my homework, ate dinner, washed dishes, and got ready for bed. Then I read in my room. I didn't sit around and chat with my family, or watch TV with them. Why would I? They didn't have time for me.

Chapter 35

WHEN HALLOWEEN CAME, MAMI SAID WE could trick-or-treat outside our building for the first time ever. "Just to Chichi's and Lydia's stores," she said. "And the library. Mrs. Rivera said she would have some treats."

Gracie wore a tie-dyed shirt, dollar-store sunglasses, and a necklace with a large peace-sign pendant. Papi lent me his Robinson Canó Yankees jersey. I was nervous about wearing it; I knew it was expensive and very special to Papi. He only wore it when he watched games, "for good luck," he said, even though Canó wasn't on the Yankees anymore. I didn't want to spill anything on it, or rip it, or damage it in any way.

"It's just a shirt, Ana María," Papi had said that morning when he took the jersey out of his closet and handed it to me. "Besides, I trust you completely. You've been an adult since the day you were born."

Rosie was doing cartwheels all over the living room. She got to wear one of her tutus from dance class to school and came home with a bagful of candy from her class party. Now she kept bumping into the couch or the coffee table. She knocked over a clay figurine of a lady in a long blue dress holding a bouquet of white and yellow flowers. Mami had bought that in the Dominican Republic, and she was not happy to see the lady's black braid crack off when it hit the edge of the table. Mami picked up the pieces and stared at them, turning them over and over. "I'm sorry," Rosie said when she was upright and realized what she had done.

"That's enough cartwheels," Mami said. "Sit down now like a civilized person."

"Anamay can fix it," Rosie said. "Right, Anamay?"

"Why me? I didn't break it."

"Because you're good at these things."

"Oh, could you, *mi amor*?" Mami put the pieces in my hand. "You can work on it later tonight."

"Okay, but I don't see what's so hard about gluing. Anybody could do it." I headed down the hall to put the pieces in my room.

I had only taken two steps when Connie jumped into me. Connie was a bunny rabbit for Halloween. Her costume—made by Mami about ten years ago—looked like fuzzy white footy pajamas with a pale pink oval belly and a headband with white-and-pink bunny ears. Connie kept hopping around the house with her arms held up in front of her, her elbows at her waist and her hands close together and bent down at the wrists. I remembered doing the same thing when I wore that costume.

When I got back to the living room, Mami clapped her hands to get our attention. "Okay, girls. Let's take a picture so Papi can see. I'm sure some of you will be covered in melted chocolate by the time he gets home from work." She held us by the shoulders and lined us up in front of the piano. When she stepped back to snap the photo, the arm-chair was in the way. "Move over a little." She motioned for us to squeeze in together, so we would be in front of the half of the piano that was not blocked by the chair.

"Will you please hurry up and take the picture?" I was tired of smiling.

"Okay, okay." Snap. "Now another one, just in case."

Too late. Rosie was already tumbling into the piano, and Connie was back to hopping. Mami gave up. Thank good-ness for the brats.

Mami plopped down on the sofa. "I'm exhausted," she said. "You girls should go now before it gets dark. And remember, Chichi's and Lydia's, the library, then back here. You can go to all the apartments on this floor and on Abuelita's floor."

"What? You're not coming with us?" I didn't want to be responsible for Rosie and Connie while they were being so crazy.

"Oh, it's okay, we can handle it. You rest, Mami." Gracie slipped a bright orange shopping bag into the crook of her arm, and handed Rosie and Connie their plastic jack-o'-lanterns.

"Oh, yeah, you say that now, but you'll ditch us when you see your friends," I said.

"Well, if you really need me to go with you—" Mami started to stand up.

"No, no, no! We're fine." Gracie grabbed Rosie and Connie by the hands and walked out the door. I took my orange shopping bag and followed them into the hallway. "What is wrong with you?" Gracie hissed at me. "Don't you see that Mami's tired?"

"Well, that's not my fault! If she wants all these kids, she should take care of them. Why should I do it for her?"

Gracie pushed the elevator down button about fifty times.

"That won't make it come any faster," I said.

She didn't look at me and kept pushing the button until the elevator finally came. It was empty. Rosie pressed the ground level button, then stood close to Gracie, leaning on her a little. "Are you mad at me?" She looked up at Gracie.

"No, not at you." Gracie looked at me, then turned her head away. Like I cared.

"Stop fighting! Stop fighting!" Connie scolded us as she hopped around the elevator. She stumbled when it came to a stop, and I leaned forward to grab her arm and steady her. Gracie didn't even move.

The elevator door opened and a woman pushed in a giant baby carriage that took up practically the whole elevator. A little boy in a cape and vampire teeth held on to the handle of the carriage. My sisters and I squeezed to one side of the elevator and listened to the baby scream the whole rest of the way down.

Outside it mostly seemed like any other day, except for a few kids in costumes here and there. Cars snaked their way around double- and triple-parked vehicles, their horns honking and music blaring out of their open windows. Chichi's and Lydia's stores were two blocks away. When we reached the first corner, I held Connie's hand and Gracie took hold of Rosie. Just as we got to the other side, two of Gracie's friends from middle school stepped out of their apartment building. "Gracie!" they shrieked.

Gracie shrieked back, "Vicky! Rebecca!" They hugged and hugged. Vicky was dressed as a "sexy cat," and Rebecca was a "sexy nurse." They had on so much makeup they looked like clowns.

"Are you going trick-or-treating?" Vicky the clown-cat looked at Gracie's orange bag like it had cooties.

Gracie rolled her eyes. "Yeah, I have to take my little sisters."

"Oh, you're so cute!" Rebecca the clown-nurse ruffled Connie's curls.

"Don't mess up my ears!" Connie backed away and reached up to straighten out her rabbit-ears headband.

"Connie, don't be rude," Gracie said. "She gave you a compliment. You need to say thank you."

Connie looked down and mumbled into her jack-o'-lantern bucket, "Thank you."

Gracie turned back to her friends. "I'm sorry about that."

"Oh, that's okay. Listen, we're going to a party at Johnny's house. You should come."

"That sounds like fun!" Gracie noticed me glaring at her. "But I can't. I promised my mom I would keep an eye on my little sisters."

"Can't Anamay watch them?"

"No," I said to Vicky, "Anamay can't watch them. Not alone. And besides, Gracie can't go to some boy's house without our parents' permission." I turned to Gracie. "Can we go now?"

Gracie looked up at the sky as though I were the troublesome one. "Okay, fine, we'll go in a minute." She started talking to Vicky and Rebecca about high school.

When I looked around, I didn't see Rosie and Connie anywhere. Finally I spotted them halfway down the block, watching a game of dominoes in front of the bodega. I ran over to them. "What are you doing? You have to stay with us!"

"You took too long," Connie said. "And I don't have candy yet!"

"Okay, well, let's wait for Gracie and then we can cross the street." I looked back at the corner. Gracie was just gabbing away with her friends. This was so typical. "Fine, we'll just go without her." I took Connie by the hand and reached for Rosie with my other hand.

"I don't want to go without Gracie," Rosie said. She folded her arms in front of her.

"Rosie, just take my hand. We'll wait for Gracie at Chichi's."

Rosie hugged herself tighter. "No. You're not in charge. Gracie's the oldest, so I don't have to listen to you."

When Rosie needed someone to walk her to a birthday party or help her with a school project, she bugged me, not Gracie, but now all of a sudden it was about who was older. I could not believe my parents were having one more annoying kid. Why didn't one or two of my sisters just disappear? That would make life so much better.

"Fine, you stay here and wait for Gracie," I said. Rosie would wait all afternoon, and she wouldn't get any candy, but that was *her* problem. The light turned green. I held on to Connie and crossed the street.

A car with duct tape all over the bumper rattled toward us. "Is that Tío Lalo?" Connie said.

Suddenly, the car swerved toward the sidewalk on the other side, which was crowded with people walking back and forth. But I saw only one: Rosie, still standing by the curb.

The car slammed into Rosie and sent her flying up into the air.

"Rosie!" Gracie screamed.

The car rammed into the streetlight, which tumbled to the ground with a vibrating clash. I barely heard it. I felt like

I was trapped inside a stone statue, trying to move. *Please, Rosie, get up. Please, please, jump up and cartwheel your way over here.* But Rosie was lying completely still in her ripped tutu on the edge of the sidewalk.

Chapter 36

I COULDN'T MOVE. PEOPLE RAN AND SHOUTED all around me, but I just stood there staring at Rosie. Gracie ran over and cradled Rosie's head in her arms, tears in her eyes. Tío Lalo knelt beside Gracie and cried too. "I'm sorry! I'm so sorry!" he said over and over again. A sudden pain in my arm made me look down.

"Let's go to Rosie!" Connie screamed as she yanked again.

I blinked a few times, then looked twice for traffic. No cars were coming since the street was littered with the twisted streetlight and pieces of my uncle's car. I forced my feet to move, and Connie and I crossed the street to be with our sisters. Rosie looked like a rag doll in Gracie's arms, with her eyes closed and her left leg all twisted into a weird shape. "Is she breathing?" I said in a whisper to Gracie. Gracie nodded, and I felt a sob creep up my throat and out of my mouth.

Chichi and Lydia came over to join us. "I called your mother," Lydia said.

"Don't worry, *mamita*. Everything will be okay," Chichi said as she held Connie and wiped her tears.

By the time Mami and Abuelita arrived, three police cars and an ambulance had arrived. One police officer grabbed Tío Lalo and made him breathe into a tube attached to a little box. Two other officers wrote in their notebooks while they spoke with Chichi, Lydia, and other adults who had seen the accident. The ambulance people put Rosie on a stretcher and told Mami and Abuelita to stand back. Still, the two of them hovered over her while they cried and cried.

The police officer cuffed Tío Lalo's hands behind his back.

"My baby!" Abuelita screamed. "My baby can't go to jail! Mecho, do something! Help your brother!"

Mami glared at Abuelita as she climbed into the ambulance with Rosie.

"Mamá, come with me!" Tío Lalo shouted.

Abuelita looked back and forth between my uncle and my sisters and me. "I—I can't," she stammered to Tío Lalo. "I promised Mecho I would watch over the girls and take them home."

"I'm not going home," I said. "I'm going to the hospital."

"Me too." Gracie stood beside me.

"But I promised your mother . . ."

"We have to go to Rosie!" I was screaming now. "We can't

213

leave her!" I lowered my voice and looked at Connie, who was still crying. "Not again," I whispered.

"Rosie! Rosie! Rosie! I want Rosie!" Connie grabbed Abuelita's hand and pulled hard with each "Rosie!"

"Mamá! Mamá!" Tío Lalo called. The officer pushed my uncle's head down and put him into the back of the police car.

Abuelita ran up to the police officer. *"Habla español?"* she asked. He nodded, and she began to plead in Spanish. "It was just an accident. He's never been in trouble with the law before. He's a good boy. Do you know that was his niece he hit? He loves her, he would never do anything to hurt her, he feels terrible about this. Can't you just let him go with a warning?"

"Driving drunk is a crime, *doña*," the officer said. "He can call you after he's booked." Abuelita watched the police car pull away. She kept staring even after it had turned a corner and couldn't be seen anymore.

"Abuelita," Gracie said. She touched Abuelita's shoulder. My grandmother turned around and reached for Gracie with both arms. The two of them held each other tightly and cried.

What were they doing? I knew Abuelita loved Rosie and was upset about this. And I knew Tío Lalo was sad too. But the two of them always acted like my uncle's drinking wasn't a problem, and now look what happened. Abuelita was as much to blame for Rosie's accident as Tío

214

Lalo was. And we really didn't have time for this. "Can we take a cab?" I asked.

Abuelita pulled away from Gracie and nodded. She wiped her face with a tissue and looked around. Chichi and Lydia were still talking to the police officers. The bodega guy came up to us. "Do you need something, *doña*?" he said to Abuelita.

"Yes, a taxi."

"My cousin drives a taxi." The bodega guy pointed to one of the domino players, who jumped up and pulled a jangle of keys out of his pocket.

"Come, *doñita*," the cousin said. "I'll take you."

We followed the man around the corner to a brown car with one blue door and one white door. We squeezed inside and rode in silence. It took us forever to get to the hospital. First, the taxi driver said his tank was almost empty, so he drove in the opposite direction to a gas station with a long line of cars waiting at the pump. When we pulled out of there, we got caught in rush-hour traffic and then had to turn around—very slowly—when we reached a street that was closed for roadwork.

The more time passed, the more I worried. I wondered what we would find when we got to the hospital. Would Rosie still be alive? Would she ever be fine again? I tried to just be mad at Tío Lalo for hitting her, at Abuelita for never discouraging his drunk driving, at Gracie for ditching us to hang out with her friends, and even at Connie for insisting

215

that we move on without Gracie. But I kept going back to being mad at myself too. If only I had stayed to wait for Gracie. If I had insisted that Rosie come with Connie and me. If I had done something differently—anything. But I didn't.

When we got to the hospital, we didn't know where to find Rosie and Mami. Gracie asked a bunch of people, but everyone was running around looking busy and telling us to wait. Finally, a smiley woman with gray hair and pink scrubs came to our rescue. "I'll take you to find your parents," she said, "but then you have to go to the waiting area, because you really shouldn't be here, especially not the little one." We thanked her and said goodbye as soon as we saw Mami and Papi slip into the hallway from a room behind a curtain.

"Mamá, I thought you were taking them home," Mami said.

"They insisted on coming," Abuelita said. "I'm sorry." She started to cry.

"That's okay," Papi said. He picked Connie up and she leaned her head on his shoulder and sobbed. "Everything's going to be okay." He patted her back and swayed from side to side.

Mami put her arms around Gracie and me. "The doctor says your sister has a concussion, a broken leg, and two fractured ribs," she said. "They gave her a lot of painkillers, so she's asleep now."

"Can we see her?" I asked.

My parents looked at each other, then shook their heads. "Not yet," Mami said.

"You stay here with Rosalba," Papi said to Mami. "I'll go to the waiting area with the girls."

Mami went back behind the curtain, and Papi led us to the waiting area with Connie in his arms. Abuelita sat down. She was still crying. Gracie sat next to her and rubbed her shoulder. "Don't worry, Abuelita," Gracie said. "She'll be okay."

"I know," Abuelita said with a sniffle. "God will protect her. Here, Tavito, I'll hold the baby."

Papi handed the sleeping Connie over to Abuelita. I sat next to Gracie and watched Papi pace in front of us.

"This is all your fault," Gracie muttered to me.

"What?!" I didn't bother to lower my voice. "You're kidding, right?" Even though I felt guilty about this, I figured Gracie would blame herself. I would if I were her.

"No, I'm not kidding. Why did you leave her on the curb?"

"Well, you left all of us! I knew you would do that. You always do that!" I was shouting now.

"You probably did it on purpose," Gracie said. "You don't care about Rosie. You don't care about any of us. That's why you burned the envelope!"

I stared at her. Why would she say that? The envelope had nothing to do with any of this. She was just trying to get me in trouble. "You promised you wouldn't tell anybody," I whispered.

"Well, I guess I lied!" Gracie folded her arms over her chest and turned away from me.

I looked at Papi. He was watching the two of us. Did he believe that I didn't care about the family? Maybe. After all, I had been kind of bratty all week. But Gracie never took care of our little sisters. She always left that to me. And now she had the nerve to accuse me of not caring! I stood up and headed for the elevators.

"Ana María, where do you think you're going?"

Papi was right behind me. An elevator door opened, and some people in white coats rushed out, almost bumping into me. I turned and faced Papi. "Gracie's right," I said. "This is all my fault. I should have stayed with Rosie." My face was wet with tears, and my glasses slid down my nose.

"This is not your fault. She was on the sidewalk, right?"

I nodded.

"Well, if you had stayed with her, all three of you would have been hit. The only person to blame here is Lalo." He started to pace again.

I looked at the floor and listened to the beeping sounds all around me. It was good to know that my parents didn't blame me for Rosie's accident. But I still blamed myself. Plus, there was this business about the envelope. "Gracie's right about the envelope," I said. "The one the doctor gave you about the baby."

Papi stopped pacing.

"It was an accident. I wanted to see what was inside, but

I had said I didn't care so I couldn't say I wanted to know, and I thought I could just steam it open real fast and then I put it too close to the fire and before I knew it, it was up in flames!" I took a deep breath.

Papi shook his head. "You forgot to close my desk drawer, and the doctor's envelope had her return address on it."

"So . . ." I said. "You knew already?"

"We knew something fishy had happened, but we didn't realize you had played with fire. That was very dangerous." Papi frowned. "I expect better from you. Your mother and I will have to talk about this."

I lowered my eyes and mumbled, "Sorry."

A voice on the loudspeaker paged a doctor, again and again. When it stopped, Papi put an arm around my shoulder. "Look, the important thing is that you and your other sisters are fine, and that Rosalba will bounce back in no time. You did a good job keeping Consuelo safe, but accidents happen. This isn't your fault, you understand?"

I looked at Papi and nodded.

"Come on, let's go back to the others," he said.

✳ ✳ ✳

Chaos had taken over the waiting area. Abuelita was making the sign of the cross and saying, "*Ay, Virgencita, por favor ayúdela!*" Then I heard Connie. "Mami! Mami!" she shrieked. Three people in scrubs were bent over someone—Mami! Papi sprinted over to her.

219

"Stand back please, sir," one of the medical people said. They lifted Mami into a wheelchair. She was awake, but her eyes were half closed and her head was wobbly. Papi followed as they wheeled her away.

"What happened?" I asked Gracie.

"Mami came out here to get Papi and then she fainted," Gracie said.

"Oh." I sat down.

Connie climbed onto my lap. "Is Mami okay?"

What could I say? I had no idea.

"It's all this worrying," Abuelita said. She walked back and forth and threw her arms up in the air. "When a pregnant woman worries, she loses the baby. *Ay, Dios mío!*" She sat down and took her rosary out of her purse. Then she closed her eyes and prayed.

Was Abuelita right? Would Mami lose the baby? And what about Rosie? I had just wished for some kids in my family to disappear. Would that wish come true? How could I have thought such a thing? Maybe Gracie was right about me. I was an awful person, and this was all my fault.

Chapter 37

Mami had to stay in the hospital overnight so the doctors could keep an eye on her blood pressure, which was super high. Papi stayed too, so Abuelita took us home. She made dinner and put Connie to bed. Then she turned to Gracie and me. "Can I trust the two of you to stay here alone tonight without killing each other?" she asked.

Gracie and I glanced at each other, then hung our heads. "Yes," we muttered.

"Good. I have some things to take care of at my house, but if you need anything, just call and I'll come right up."

Gracie and I didn't talk all evening. I glued together the clay figurine Rosie had broken earlier in the day, while Gracie texted with I didn't know who. We were careful not to bump into each other while we cleaned up the kitchen, and we took turns in the bathroom without fighting about it.

I couldn't sleep. I lay on my back and listened to Gracie toss and turn above me and to Connie snoring in her new bed beside me. I remembered Rosie's first night in her top bunk. She had been so fidgety that Gracie kept shushing her and telling her to be still. How would Rosie get up there now?

I pulled out my glasses and put them on, then I got out of bed and stripped off the sheets. Gracie lifted herself up onto her elbows and watched me. When I reached for Rosie's sheets, Gracie got down and helped me. After my sheets were on Rosie's top bunk, and Rosie's were on my bottom bunk, I climbed up into my new bed and lay down.

"I'm sorry for telling about the envelope," Gracie said.

"It's okay," I said. "They already knew."

"What? How?"

"They had figured it out. Our parents aren't as dumb as they look."

Gracie giggled. "Also, I'm sorry for ditching you with Rosie and Connie," she said.

"Well, we should have been more patient. I know you don't get to see Vicky and Rebecca now that you're in that new school."

"Thanks, but I shouldn't have left you." We were quiet for a little while. "Do you think Mami and Rosie will be okay?" Gracie said. I could hear the fear in her voice. It was the same fear I was feeling.

"Yes, of course," I said. I had to believe that. I just had to.

✳ ✳ ✳

When I woke up the next morning, I thought: *This is the worst birthday ever.* I could hear Abuelita in the kitchen making breakfast, so I went to see if she had any news about Mami and Rosie. "Your father called," she said to me. "He said you can stay home from school today, but make sure you go to your piano lesson." Gracie already had the day off because it was All Saints' Day. Usually, I would rather go to school than sit around at home, but I hadn't slept well the night before, so I took a long nap after breakfast.

That afternoon I walked to Doña Dulce's house with my head down. I sat at the piano and started with scales. I had practiced my recital piece every day that week, and I had been sure Doña Dulce would be super happy with my progress. But I kept messing up.

"What's the matter, Anamay?" Doña Dulce said. "Your head doesn't seem to be in it today."

I took my hands off the piano and put them on my lap. "Mami and Rosie are in the hospital," I said.

"Oh my goodness, what happened?"

"Rosie was hit by a car yesterday, and she has a concussion, a broken leg, and two fractured ribs." I kept my eyes on my hands. I didn't want Doña Dulce to see the tears rolling down my cheeks. "And Papi said Mami has high blood pressure, so they kept her in the hospital overnight for observation, but Abuelita says she might lose the baby." *And it's all my fault.*

"Oh, sweetie, I'm so sorry!" Doña Dulce reached over and pulled me toward her.

Someone behind us cleared their throat. It was Sarita. "Anamay, is there anything I can do to help?"

"Yes," Doña Dulce said. "Tell us how we can help."

I shrugged. What could anyone do? My family and I just had to deal with this on our own.

* * *

When I got back from my piano lesson, Connie raced down the hall and into the living room to greet me. "Mami and Rosie are home!" she said. She jumped up and down.

I looked at Papi. "Really?"

Papi nodded. "Like I told your sisters, your mother is on bed rest until the doctor says otherwise, so don't bother her. But"—he pointed at me—"she wants to see you now."

I ran down the hall to Mami's room. Mami was in bed. "Look," I said. "I fixed this for you." I held up the repaired clay figurine.

"*Ay, gracias, mi amor.*" Mami reached for the figurine and examined the braid. "It's perfect." She put the figurine on her night table. "Now, open that top drawer." She pointed at her dresser.

I opened the drawer and looked inside. A box wrapped in paper with balloons all over it was on top. "Is this for me?" I said.

Mami laughed. "Of course it's for you. Happy birthday, *mamita*."

I thought everyone had forgotten about my birthday. But I should have known Mami would never forget. I took out the gift and unwrapped it. Inside was a sparkly red headband.

"It's for you to wear to Lincoln Center," Mami said.

"It's beautiful." I blinked back my tears. "Thank you, Mami." I gave her a hug. "I'm sorry I got mad at you last week," I said. "I promise I won't upset you anymore, so you don't get sick again."

"*Ay*, Anamay, this isn't your fault." Mami held me close. "Sometimes these things happen with pregnancies, especially when a woman is a little older."

That was a relief. Sort of. "So, something might still go wrong?" I asked.

"Well, something can always go wrong," Mami said. "That's just life. But we're going to follow the doctor's instructions and everything will probably be fine."

I nodded. That made sense. "It's okay if you don't come to Lincoln Center," I said. "I know you don't like piano recitals."

Mami looked at me and crinkled her eyebrows together. "Why would you think that?"

I shrugged. "You just don't seem to like my piano playing very much. I mean, you always leave the room when I practice. But that's okay."

"Anamay, I love hearing you play! I don't stay to listen because I need to take your little sisters away so they won't bother you."

Hmm. That made sense. Maybe instead of being mad at Mami for hanging out with my sisters, I should have been thanking her for helping me concentrate on my practicing.

Mami reached up and stroked my cheek. "I know we don't do a lot together, and it makes me a little sad to know that I can't teach you anything. I don't know anything about music, and my English isn't good enough to read all those books you like." Her eyes teared up. "You're so smart and independent. I want to be there for you if you need me, but I feel like you've outgrown me."

I couldn't believe what I was hearing. I had always thought Mami just didn't like spending time with me. "I'll never outgrow you," I said. "And there are lots of things I want you to teach me."

Mami sat up straighter and smiled. "Really? Like what?"

"Like how to read that Spanish book Tía Nona gave me. It's really hard and there are a bunch of words I don't understand."

"I've always wanted to read *Don Quixote*," Mami said. "I'd love to help you with it."

Mami and I were hugging again when Papi walked in holding a wrapped gift and a large yellow envelope.

"Happy birthday, Ana María." Papi handed me the present and envelope. I unwrapped the package. It was a

Chopin and Liszt CD. "Your recital song is on there. Of course, it doesn't sound as good as when you play it."

I laughed and thanked my father. Then I opened the envelope. Inside was a card from Tía Nona with a check for fifty dollars. There were also a few sheets of piano music with the title "Quisqueyanos Valientes."

"Oh, that's the Dominican national anthem," Mami said. There was a note stapled on top. In big letters, someone had written: *You can play this the next time we're together. From, CLARISA.*

"That's nice of her," Papi said, looking over my shoulder. It *was* nice. And I was super glad she wasn't mad at me anymore.

I turned back to Papi. "I just told Mami this, but it's okay if the two of you can't go to the Lincoln Center recital," I said. "I know you want to, but if the baby comes that day, that's not your fault. And Doña Dulce said the showcase people will sell a DVD of the show if we want to get that."

"Oh, we should buy the DVD no matter what," Mami said. "I want to have that memory forever."

"Absolutely!" Papi said. "Now, it's time for your mother to rest."

I left my parents and went into my room to hang out with Rosie. She was lying on my old bed. One of her cheeks was bruised, and her left leg was in a bright blue cast. She was holding an ice pack against her chest. I wanted to hug her, but I was afraid I might hurt her. "How do you feel?" I asked.

"I can't watch TV!" Rosie said. "Or read or use a computer. All because of this stupid concussion!" It was good to see her pout and hear her complain. She might be a little battered, but she was still the same old Rosie.

"What can you do?" I said.

"Just listen to stuff. Like music and other people reading."

"I can play the piano for you and read to you."

Rosie smiled. "Yeah! Will you read to me now?"

The buzzer sounded. When Papi opened the apartment door, Rosie and I heard Chichi's voice in the living room. "Here's a lasagna for your dinner tonight," she said.

"Oh, you shouldn't have," Papi said.

"Of course I should!" Chichi said. "And Lydia's making you something tomorrow. So don't worry about a thing; we'll take care of you just like you and Mecho have always taken care of us."

Gracie and I ate in our room with Rosie, and Papi and Connie kept Mami company. After dinner, Papi and Gracie cleaned up the kitchen while I read to Rosie. Connie would not leave Mami's side. I had been reading for about an hour when Papi rolled in his desk chair. "Your mother wants to spend a little time with you girls," he said. Mami leaned on Papi as she walked in the room and sat down on the chair. Connie curled up next to me on the floor and giggled with her hand over her mouth.

"What's so funny?" I asked.

"Oh, nothing," Connie said.

I looked up and saw Gracie in the doorway holding a plate of cupcakes. The middle cupcake had a candle in it. She walked in and my family sang "Happy Birthday" to me. This was the happiest I had ever felt on my birthday. We were all together, and just that morning I had wondered if we ever would be again. I closed my eyes and made a wish. Then I blew out the candle.

Chapter 38

*P*API STAYED HOME FROM WORK THE rest of the week. "You need some help," Gracie told him on the first day. "I'll stay home too."

"Absolutely not," Papi said. "We'll be fine. Go to school."

"But —"

"No buts! Go."

Gracie huffed all the way back to our room.

"Do you have a test or something today?" I asked.

"No," Gracie said. She slipped on her uniform skirt. "Why?"

"I'm just wondering why you don't want to go to school."

"Because Papi obviously needs us!"

"Abuelita said she'd come over later. Besides, Mami will worry if we don't go to school, so the best thing we can do for her is go."

Gracie finished dressing and picked up her backpack.

"You just say that because you're a nerd and you love school," she said.

I looked at Gracie for a few seconds, then I got up and went to the bathroom. I didn't want to argue with her anymore.

* * *

Tío Lalo was in our living room when I got home that afternoon. Abuelita must have told him to clean himself up before coming over. He looked like a wet puppy with his hair slicked back and his big sad eyes. "I'm so sorry, Tavito," he said to Papi. "I promise I will never, ever, ever drink again."

Papi snorted. "Just don't drive when you drink, okay?"

Tío Lalo nodded like a bobblehead doll.

Papi handed him a business card. "This is the best criminal lawyer I know," he said. "She's usually very expensive, but she'll help you for free as a favor to Mecho and me."

"Thank you! Thank you!" Tío Lalo said. "You won't regret this. I promise."

Papi opened the apartment door. "I need to give Mecho her medicine now."

"Oh . . . can I see her? I want to apologize."

"No, she doesn't want to see you right now." Papi opened the door a little wider.

"Oh." Tío Lalo gulped. His Adam's apple moved up and back down. He turned back to Papi like he just had a great idea. "Can I say hello to Rosita? I can cheer her up. You know I always make her laugh!"

"Laughing isn't a good idea right now. With her broken ribs, that just causes more pain."

Tío Lalo looked at me. I shrugged. "Okay, well, I'll see all of you later, then," Tío Lalo said. "Give my love to Mecho and the rest of the girls." He waved the business card in his hand. "And thanks again."

"Is that Claudia's mom's card?" I asked Papi after he closed the door behind Tío Lalo.

"Yes."

"Did Mami really say she doesn't want to see Tío Lalo?"

"She did." Papi walked into the kitchen.

I followed him. "Wow, does Abuelita know?"

Papi took two glasses out of the cupboard. He chuckled. "She does. Could you take the orange juice out, please? Your mother is so mad at Lalo she practically hisses if anyone mentions his name." Papi poured juice into the glasses and handed me a bottle of pills, a bottle of liquid medicine, and a spoon. "Here, take these back to our room." He picked up the two glasses of orange juice and walked behind me. "I think your grandmother is afraid of her now."

Rosie and Connie were in bed with Mami. Papi handed one glass to Mami and one to Rosie. He gave Mami her pills and fed a spoonful of medicine to Rosie. "Okay, Rosalba, it's three o'clock now," Papi said. "You know what that means."

"Do I have to?" Rosie said.

"Yes, you do."

"But I don't want to."

"I know, but remember what the doctor said, right?" Papi took Rosie's hand and squeezed it. "If you don't take a deep breath once an hour, you might get pneumonia or a collapsed lung."

"But it hurts!"

"Come on, *mamita*," Mami said. "It's for your own good."

Rosie sat up and gulped in a mouthful of air. She closed her eyes and whimpered while she breathed out. Connie buried her face in Mami's chest and cried. I blinked hard and turned my head away.

"Good girl," Papi said.

Mami smoothed down Rosie's hair. "See, that wasn't so bad, right?"

Rosie pouted. "Can you play something for me, Anamay?"

Papi carried Rosie into the living room and settled her onto the couch. I played the piano until she fell asleep. Then I went to ask Papi for a favor. "Could you order this for me?" I showed him a picture of a harmonica on the computer. "I'll use my birthday money from Tía Nona."

"Sure," Papi said, "but I didn't know you were interested in the harmonica."

"It's not for me. I want to send it to Clarisa, so she can have her own musical instrument."

Papi smiled. "That's a great idea." The price of the harmonica and the cost of shipping added up to about half of my birthday money. The rest went into my college fund, as always. Sending the harmonica to Clarisa was my birthday present to myself. I hoped she liked it too.

Chapter 39

OVER THE NEXT FEW WEEKS, OUR house felt like a restaurant, with all the people in the neighborhood as our chefs and waiters. Chichi made up a calendar and people signed up to help us. Mrs. Jiménez took over our kitchen on Mondays and Thursdays, when she made so much food that Mami, Rosie, and Connie ate the leftovers for lunch the next day. Chichi and Lydia took turns on Wednesdays and Fridays, and a different person from church would bring over a casserole each Tuesday. Ruben and Mrs. Rivera took care of weekends. Claudia's parents sent us giant boxes of fruit once a week. Sometimes someone who wasn't even on the calendar would show up with dessert or a loaf of bread, a carton of orange juice, or some milk and eggs, just because they were nearby and thinking of us. We had to invite people to join us for meals because we had way too much food to finish on our own.

Not all of our helpers cooked. Millie showed up super

early one Saturday morning without Max or the baby. "They're still asleep," she said. Her eyes were red and had puffy, gray half-moons underneath them. "Let's get to work." Millie emptied the laundry hampers into Mami's shopping cart. She took the sheets off our beds and squished them on top of the clothes. Gracie grabbed the detergent and the quarters, and they did our laundry together.

Sarita and Lucy also came over that day. Lucy's baby wore a little crocheted hat Mami had made for him. "Oh, how adorable!" Mami said. She sat on the couch with her feet up. "May I hold him?" Lucy handed him over.

"This is from Doña Dulce," Sarita said. She gave Papi a big round plastic container. "It's black beans. Her specialty, she says."

Papi thanked her. "We'll call Doña Dulce later," he said. "Where are the boys?"

"Believe it or not, they're with Doña Dulce," Lucy said. "We hope they don't destroy her house."

"Or drive her crazy," Sarita said.

"Or both!"

Sarita and Lucy helped us clean. Lucy did the bathroom, while Sarita and I vacuumed and dusted. Then Rosie asked Sarita to play something on the piano for her.

"Don't bother Sarita with that," I said. "I can play for you."

"But I want to hear Sarita play!"

"Fine," I said. But it wasn't fine. Why wasn't my playing good enough for my sister?

"I'll just play a short minuet by Bach," Sarita said. "Lucy has to put the baby down for a nap soon."

Lucy's baby must have heard that, because he started to cry and wouldn't stop.

"Oh well," I said. "I guess you have to go now. You can play for us another time."

"No, Sarita, go ahead and play," Mami said. "Let's take the baby to my room, Lucy."

Connie followed Mami and Lucy to the bedroom. Papi had gone to the drugstore, and Gracie was still in the laundry room with Millie, so it was just Rosie and me watching Sarita play. I hardly ever got a quiet moment to practice, and now my one chance was being hogged by Sarita.

Sarita sat down at the piano and started to play Minuet in G Major. I recognized the piece right away because I had learned it a while ago and had played it many times before. But, as always, Sarita's version sounded different. Better. So much better. And, as always, I couldn't breathe or move while she played.

Rosie clapped when Sarita finished. Sarita looked over at her and smiled. There were tears in Sarita's eyes.

"Are you okay?" I asked.

Sarita nodded. "Bach always reminds me of my mother. He was just a little kid when his mother died."

Rosie's eyes opened wide. "Did your mother die too?"

"Rosie!" I said. "It's not polite to ask such a personal question."

"It's okay," Sarita said. "You're my friends."

I had never thought of Sarita as a friend before, probably because the only time I ever saw her was on Tuesday afternoons. And sometimes I didn't even see her, I only heard her playing.

Sarita pulled at a loose thread hanging from her jeans. "My mother didn't die. She loves us. I know she does. She can't help it that she's addicted to drugs." She looked at me like she expected me to say something mean about her mom, like she was ready to defend her if I did. A lot of people probably criticized Sarita's mom, but I knew better. Sometimes family members can have problems—like Tío Lalo—but that doesn't mean you stop loving one another.

Sarita looked back at the piece of thread between her fingers. "Papi kicked her out last year. He changed the locks and everything. All because we came home one day and the house was empty. She had sold everything for drug money. Even my little brothers' shoes."

Rosie's mouth hung open. I hoped she wouldn't say anything rude.

"Sometimes she comes over and begs us to let her in so she can shower and take a nap. But Papi won't let her! I know she loves me! I know she does." Sarita yanked at the thread and ripped it in two.

What would it be like to have a mother who didn't take care of you? I couldn't imagine what Sarita was feeling. I couldn't imagine what she felt every day. I sat on the piano bench next to Sarita and put my arms around her. My friend leaned her head on my shoulder and sobbed.

Chapter 40

Two weeks after the accident, Rosie's dance teacher came to visit. She brought a bouquet of pink and white carnations. In the very center of the flowers, hovering above them, was a plastic ballerina with her leg extended behind her in an arabesque. "These are from the whole class," she said to Rosie. "We all miss you so much!"

"How sweet!" Mami said from her seat on the couch.

"Thank you, Mrs. Santana!" Rosie said. It was good to see her smile. Ever since the accident, she was itching to get up, run, and dance. She was so bored that she didn't even complain about doing the homework her teacher emailed to Papi each day. "I miss everybody too," she said, "so, so much!"

"And that's not all the class got for you," Mrs. Santana said. She handed Rosie a long brown envelope. "It's for you and your family."

Rosie peeked inside the envelope and pulled out several slips of paper. Her eyes opened wide as she read the top one. "A ticket to *The Nutcracker*?"

Mrs. Santana nodded. "Five of them," she said. She looked at Mami. "I hope that's okay; it's in a few weeks and I assumed you wouldn't be able to go."

"You assumed right," Mami said. "Besides, this is beyond generous! How can we thank you?"

"Just get better and come back to class," Mrs. Santana said to Rosie. Rosie hugged her teacher and then waved her arms up in the air. She had been doing that a lot lately. Her arm dance.

* * *

Mami was knitting all the time now that she was on bed rest. She was just as restless as Rosie. "I can't believe I have to stay in bed until the baby comes," she said. "That's more than a month away!" Abuelita came over every day to take care of Mami, Rosie, and Connie while Papi, Gracie, and I were gone. I didn't know what they talked about while I was at school, but I never heard my grandmother mention Tío Lalo. I sort of wanted to ask about him, but I thought that might upset Mami. I knew he wasn't in jail because Claudia told me her mom helped him avoid jail time. Instead he had to pay a fine, do community service, and go to rehab. Claudia didn't know if it was all working out, though, and I hoped it was. I was still mad at him, but I missed how happy Abuelita seemed when he was around. She had always said that a tight-knit family is the most important thing in the world. It was probably tough for her to see one of her kids not talking to another one. But she never brought up his name.

Rosie finally went back to school the Monday before Thanksgiving. "Look, everybody signed my cast!" she said when she got home. "And I get to use the elevator, and one of my friends can come with me to carry my books, and everyone was fighting over who got to help me!"

Mami laughed. "It sounds like you had a good day," she said.

Chichi didn't put Thanksgiving on the calendar of helpers. She and Lydia came over early that day with a turkey, string beans, and mashed potatoes with gravy. Abuelita and her friend Doña Paula were already in our kitchen cooking *pernil*, yucca, rice, and beans. "Dominican-style Thanksgiving," Abuelita called it.

The intercom buzzed all day, and everyone who arrived stayed to eat. Mr. and Mrs. Jiménez showed up with another turkey and a small plastic grocery bag. "I'm going to whip up a flan," Mrs. Jiménez said. She handed the baby to her husband and headed for the kitchen.

"Can I help, Mrs. Jiménez?" Rosie was sitting on the love seat complaining about being bored every few minutes.

"Of course, sweetie," Mrs. Jiménez said.

Rosie leaned on me and hobbled to the dining room

table. We set her up with a big bowl, a whisk, and half a dozen eggs.

Mrs. Rivera and Ruben brought a plantain-and-ground-beef casserole. "Mmm, my favorite," I said.

"Me too!" Ruben pointed at himself.

Pedro slinked in behind his mom. He carried a giant pan of sweet potatoes. Papi shook Pedro's hand. "Welcome back, young man. And stay out of my daughter's room." Papi grinned when he said that, so Pedro laughed. But he didn't go anywhere near our room. Gracie smiled all day anyway.

Even Claudia and her parents came. "We brought pies!" Claudia said. There were six of them: apple, pumpkin, and sweet potato. Two of each.

"We figured there would be a big crowd here," Claudia's dad said. "We know how Gustavo Reyes loves to party!"

Papi laughed and slapped Claudia's dad on the back, then pulled him in for a hug.

I helped Mami get dressed. "It sounds like a party out there," she said to me.

"Oh, it is."

I held Mami's hand as we walked down the hallway to the living room. She put her hands over her mouth when she saw everyone and all the food. "I should get sick more often!" she said.

We all laughed and dug in.

✳ ✳ ✳

When I woke up the day after Thanksgiving, I heard muffled voices through the wall next to my bed. I put my hand under my pillow and felt around for my glasses case. When I could see clearly, I looked around. Rosie and Connie were sound asleep, but Gracie's bed was empty. I climbed down from my bunk and stepped out into the hallway.

Gracie's voice was loud and clear behind my parents' closed door. "I can finish it," she said. "I'm sure I can."

"No, *mi amor*," Mami said. "There's still a lot to do, with very little time, and the zipper is especially tricky."

"So what are you saying?" Gracie's voice got high and shrieky. "That we're not even going to try? That Anamay's not getting her dress?"

"I'm saying that if you make a mistake there won't be any turning back."

Gracie threw the door open and plowed right into me. We stared at each other for a second, then she marched past me and down the hallway. I turned to walk away. I didn't want Mami to think I was spying on them.

Too late. "Ana María, come in here please." Papi held the door open.

I stepped inside.

"You probably heard me and Gracie," Mami said.

I nodded. I couldn't show up at Lincoln Center in one of my church dresses. The Eleanor School wouldn't want someone who didn't even know what to wear to perform at a concert. So I couldn't go. *No big deal*, I told myself. The important thing was that Mami and the baby were well. Mami wasn't ready to get up and sew, and I understood that. After all, it was just a recital. And maybe my application and exam score were so good that I could get a full scholarship anyway. I really believed all these things, but still, my throat felt dry and I had to blink again and again to keep the moisture inside my eyes.

"As you know," Papi said, "your mother has not been able to sew all month." He put his hands in his pockets and looked at the floor. "I know you've had your heart set on wearing that beautiful dress to the recital, but I think we're going to have to buy you another one."

I looked at Papi, then at Mami. "Wait, what? You're going to buy me a new dress?"

"Yes, I'm sorry, *mamita*. It won't be as nice as the one we were making for you, but there's no other choice."

Were they kidding? This was wonderful news. "But how can we afford it?" I asked.

"We'll put it on the credit card," Papi said.

"Isn't that just for emergencies?"

Mami and Papi looked at each other and smiled. "Anamay," Mami said. "This is an emergency."

I tried not to smile too big. After all, I was supposed to be upset. But I was so happy I wanted to squeal and run around the house. "So . . . when will we get this dress?"

"Sometime this weekend," Papi said. "We can bring Altagracia with us. She'll help you pick out something nice."

"Okay," I said. I wasn't crazy about the idea of Gracie coming along, but it didn't really matter. I was getting a new dress, so now I was definitely going to Lincoln Center!

* * *

Lydia and Chichi didn't sell formal gowns, but Gracie did some research online and said Macy's had some nice, affordable choices. So she, Papi, and I took the subway downtown the next day.

I tried on six dresses. One was over the price limit Papi gave us, but Gracie snuck it into the fitting room anyway. "Maybe when Papi sees how good it looks, he'll say to heck with that limit," she said. But it didn't look that good. We picked out a dark green velvety dress with rhinestones on the waist and neckline. "Very Christmassy," Gracie said. "I approve. Now you need shoes."

Papi said he hadn't planned on buying shoes too.

"You don't expect her to go barefoot, do you?" Gracie said. "I mean, you would have bought her shoes anyway, right?"

Papi closed his eyes and pinched the bridge of his nose with two fingers. "All right, let's go to the shoe store."

Having Gracie around wasn't so bad after all.

Chapter 41

ABUELITA JOINED US FOR DINNER THE night before *The Nutcracker*. "What time should we leave tomorrow?" Gracie asked Papi.

Papi rubbed his chin. "Let's see, it starts at three so we should try to get there by two thirty. On a Saturday afternoon, there might be a wait for the train . . ."

"Is it okay if Abuelita goes instead of me?" I said.

My whole family stared at me. Rosie spoke first. "Why?"

"Because . . ." I looked at my plate and poked the rice with my fork. How could I explain this? "I'm really nervous about the recital. It's only two weeks away, and I'm still not ready!" I put my fork down and sat back. "It's really nice that everyone is helping us with stuff. But there are always people here and it's hard to concentrate when I play the piano. If I stay here instead of going to the ballet, I can practice."

"Well . . ." Mami looked at Papi. He shrugged. "If that's what you really want."

"But I've heard you play that piece a million times," Gracie said. "It's perfect!"

"No, it's not," I said. "Doña Dulce says it still needs work." I knew my piano teacher was right. Sometimes when I played "Meine Freuden" I had to look at the music and double-check the notes. That was definitely not good enough for a recital. I was determined to get it just right.

"All right, then it's settled. Your *abuela* will go in your place." Papi looked at Abuelita. "Is that okay with you?"

Abuelita clapped a hundred times. "I've never been to a ballet before!" She stood up, grabbed my face with both hands, and planted a sloppy kiss on my forehead.

Mami chuckled. "I guess that's a yes." She leaned forward and wiped the lipstick off my forehead with her napkin.

✳ ✳ ✳

After everyone left for the ballet the next day, Mami went to her room to lie down. I sat at the piano, closed my eyes, and played. If I could play my piece perfectly without looking at the keys, maybe I would be ready.

After practicing for about an hour, I still kept messing up in the same spot. I stopped and looked through the sheet music to study the passage again.

A weird grunting sound cut through the sudden silence. What was that? It sounded like an angry dog or even a tiger or something. I turned my head sideways and leaned my ear toward the hallway. The animal was growling. Was it in the bedroom with Mami? Was it attacking her? I dropped the papers and ran down the hallway. The growling got louder. I burst into Mami's room.

But there was no animal there, just Mami. The noises were coming from her. She was on the bed on her hands and knees, and her eyes were closed. She let out a long, deep moan. I tiptoed toward her. "Mami?"

Mami lifted her head and looked at me. Her nose and cheeks were covered with tiny moist beads. "I think the baby's coming soon." She sucked in a deep breath and let out another animal moan.

"Now?" I said. "But the baby's not due for another three weeks."

Mami rested her head on her arms. Her chest heaved like she had just run a marathon.

I realized there was no point in arguing with Mami about this. I couldn't stop whatever was happening. And it was 3:10, so the show had already started, and Papi had surely turned off his phone. I went into the kitchen and found the phone number for Mami's doctor on the refrigerator.

"Hello? My mother's having her baby now," I said. "What should I do?"

"Who is this?"

"My mother is Dr. Miranda's patient. Her name is Mercedes Reyes."

"Oh, okay, sweetie. How far apart are her contractions?"

"Um, I don't know," I said. I remembered my parents timing contractions when Connie was born, but I didn't know how to do that, and I just wanted to get Mami to the doctor! "But my mother is moaning and sweating and she's in a lot of pain, so could you please help me!"

The lady on the other end was quiet for a second. "Could you put your mother on the phone, sweetie?"

Was she for real? I huffed and walked into the bedroom with the phone in my hand. "Mami, the lady at the doctor's office wants to talk to you."

I held the phone to Mami's ear. I could hear the woman's buzzing voice on the other end. Mami said "uh-huh" a lot. Then she moaned right into the phone. It served that lady right.

When I put the phone back to my ear, the lady said, "Sweetie, you'd better call 9-1-1. The doctor will meet you at the hospital."

The 9-1-1 operator said he would send someone out right away. "I'll stay on the phone with you," he said. "Just in case you have to deliver the baby yourself. I'll talk you through it."

"Okaaaay," I said. Did he really just say that? I couldn't deliver a baby! I gulped at the air, but I couldn't seem to breathe.

Mami started to cry. "*Ay*, Anamay, what if something goes wrong?"

I put my hand on Mami's back. She seemed so scared, and she was obviously in pain. I was scared too, but Mami needed me. I had to be strong for her. "Nothing will go wrong," I said. "We can do this." I turned back to the 9-1-1 man. "Tell me what to do," I said to him.

First the man told me I had to get Mami to lie on her side. Mami didn't want to, but I reached my arms all the way around her and held her tight. "Everything's going to be fine," I said in her ear. "Just calm down and breathe." Then I eased her off her knees and onto her side.

"You should get some clean towels," the 9-1-1 man said when I got back on the phone. "You'll need to clean the baby and keep him warm."

I jumped when the knocking started on the apartment door. "I'll be right back," I said to Mami, then ran down the hall, the phone still in my hand. No one had buzzed the intercom, but maybe someone else let the paramedics in? I looked through the peephole and saw a woman and a man in ambulance uniforms. Thank goodness. They rushed in as soon as I opened the door. "She's down here." I led the way to Mami's bedroom.

The paramedics took over right away. I thanked the 9-1-1 man and hung up, then stood back and wiped the sweat from my forehead.

"There's no time," one of the paramedics said to the other. "She'll have to deliver here."

"Anamay, don't leave me," Mami said.

I held Mami's hand and counted out loud every time she pushed. I thought it would all be over after the first push, but it wasn't. Mami kept pushing and pushing. I stayed by her head, not wanting to see what was going on down where the paramedics were looking. I watched their faces the whole time, to see if they seemed worried or scared, and to decide how worried I should be. But they just looked like they were concentrating on a tough math problem. Was that good or bad? I couldn't tell. Would the baby be tiny and sickly since it was coming so early? And what about Mami? Was her blood pressure high again? I had read books where women died while giving birth. But that was in the olden days, right? I told myself not to think about that. Nothing bad would happen.

When I blew out the candle on my birthday, I had wished for Mami to get well and have a healthy baby. My wish had to come true.

Finally, we heard the baby cry. "You have a beautiful baby girl, ma'am," one of the paramedics said. She put the baby on Mami's belly and started to scrub her clean.

I let go of the breath I had been holding in and looked at the clock radio on Mami's dresser. It was 4:37. This had been the longest hour and a half of my life.

"Do you want to try to nurse her now?" the paramedic asked after she had cut the umbilical cord and wrapped the baby in a blanket. Mami nodded, and the paramedic slid the baby up to Mami's chest. She was kind of slimy and wrinkly, but still amazing. And it didn't really matter that she was a girl. A boy would have been just as adorable. The baby opened her mouth and nursed with fast gulps.

"That's a hungry baby," I said. Mami and I laughed. And cried.

Chapter 42

I TEXTED PAPI ON MAMI'S PHONE: *Baby born at home. Meet us at the hospital. —Ana María*

Mami already had a packed bag in the closet. I grabbed it and followed the paramedic who wheeled her out of the apartment on a stretcher. The other paramedic had already raced ahead with the baby in her arms. I locked the door behind me. Both locks.

The inside of the ambulance looked like a tiny doctor's office, with bright lights overhead and sterile medical tools in cabinets with clear doors. The paramedics strapped the stretcher to the side, then put the baby in a little car seat right behind Mami. One paramedic chatted about the weather and traffic as we rolled along. I held Mami's hand and nodded and smiled at the paramedic. I figured everything was probably fine now, but I was still a little concerned. After all, there was a reason we were going to the hospital, right? I didn't ask any questions, though. Mami looked super tired, and I didn't want her to worry.

Everything happened crazy fast when we arrived at the hospital. I followed Mami into a room where her doctor was already waiting. The baby had somehow gotten to the room before us, and a doctor was looking her over. "Why is she crying so much?" I asked. "Does that hurt her?" The doctor was poking and tugging at her kind of roughly, and I needed to protect my baby sister.

"No, she's just getting used to her new lungs," the doctor said without even looking at me. A nurse came over and took my arm.

"Why don't you wait outside, sweetie," she said. "We have to examine your mom now." I looked at Mami and she nodded at me.

"Go see if your father is here yet," she said.

When Papi, Abuelita, and my sisters got to the hospital, I was still outside Mami's room. "They're examining her and the baby," I said.

Papi knocked on the door, then walked in without waiting for an answer. He closed the door behind him.

"Anamay, what happened?" Gracie asked.

"The baby couldn't wait."

"Is it a boy or a girl?" Abuelita asked.

"A girl."

"Yay!" Rosie said. She couldn't do her arm dance while she leaned on her crutches, so she did a little hand dance instead.

"Yay!" Connie copied Rosie.

The door opened. The doctors and the nurse walked out. "Come on in, ladies," Papi said.

We tiptoed in. Mami smiled at us and pointed to the bassinet next to her bed. She still looked tired, but also calm and relieved. The baby was wrapped in a striped blanket. Her eyes were closed, and her little mouth was puckered up and moving like she was still tasting her last meal.

Connie walked up to the bassinet and leaned in close to the baby's face. "Oh, how cute," she said.

"Not so close," Papi said. He pulled her back a little.

Connie turned to Papi and frowned. "But I'm the big sister!"

"I know, but we don't want to wake her, okay?"

"Come sit with me," Mami said to Connie.

That got Connie's mind off the baby. She climbed up on the bed with Mami.

"I'm so sorry I wasn't there with you, Mecho," Abuelita said.

"That's okay, everything worked out fine," Mami said. "Anamay was so calm and took such good care of me." She reached over, took my hand, and pulled me close to her.

"I'm glad I wasn't there," Gracie said. "I would have freaked out."

"I wouldn't have been much better," Abuelita said.

"Oh, I know it," Mami said. "You would have run around the house screaming."

Abuelita laughed. "I think you're right." She put her arm around my shoulder. "God knows how to take care of us," she said. "And He took care of you by giving you Anamay."

"Yes, she's my level-headed, responsible girl. I don't know what would have happened if she hadn't been there."

I felt my face get warm. It was a little embarrassing to have Mami and Abuelita go on and on like that about me, but it also felt kind of nice. And, not to brag, but they were right. No one else in my family would have done what I did. I helped keep Mami and my new little sister safe, and I was proud of myself.

"Can we stop talking about Anamay?" Rosie had made herself comfortable in an armchair in the corner of the room. "What's the baby's name?"

My parents looked at each other. "We never did choose a girl's name," Papi said. "But whatever you want is fine with me, Mecho." He leaned over the baby. She was making gurgling noises. "She's awake now." He picked her up.

"Can I hold her, Papi?" Gracie asked.

"Okay, but be careful with her head." Papi transferred the baby into Gracie's arms slowly, but stayed right next to them.

"Why don't you pick a name, Anamay?" Mami said.

"Me?" Did my parents really trust me with a big decision like that?

"I think that's a great idea," Papi said. "After all, you've known her the longest." He chuckled.

"Well . . . what about a name that reminds us of the DR?"

I said. "Like . . . Marisol, for the warm sea and bright sun."

Mami smiled and looked around the room at the rest of the family. "Marisol. I like it. Yes, I really like it."

Papi nodded. Gracie held the baby closer and spoke softly to her. "Hello there, baby Marisol," she said.

"I want to hold Marisol now!" Rosie called from her seat.

"Me too, me too!" Connie jumped off the bed.

Abuelita sat on the edge of Mami's bed, and the three of us watched my sisters argue over who would hold Marisol next. Mami smiled and held my hand.

Then I looked up and saw Tío Lalo standing by the door. He clutched a white teddy bear and a bundle of red and yellow roses. A brown shopping bag hung from his wrist. "Hey," he said.

"Tío Lalo!" Connie ran to him and grabbed his free hand. "I'm a big sister!"

Tío Lalo got down on one knee and faced Connie. "Well, congratulations, you big girl! I'm so proud of you!"

"Come see my baby sister!" Connie dragged Tío Lalo toward Gracie. Tío Lalo laughed and let Connie lead him. Then he saw Rosie's cast and his smile disappeared.

"Rosita, I'm so sorry." Tío Lalo blinked and blinked, and then gulped.

"That's okay, Tío. I know you didn't mean it."

"Oh, I really, really didn't," Tío Lalo said. "How do you feel?"

"I'm better. And I forgive you. But"—Rosie wagged a

finger at Tío Lalo—"don't ever do that again!"

Tío Lalo laughed and cried at the same time. He went to Rosie and hugged her. "I promise—I cross my heart and hope to die." Then he looked at Mami. He did not step toward her. "I'm in rehab now, Mecho. This was a real wake-up call for me." Tears streamed down his face and he twisted the teddy bear's leg. "I love your girls so much. I never want to hurt them—again. I am so sorry. Can you forgive me?"

Mami closed her eyes. We watched her and waited. And waited some more. Then she opened her eyes and nodded once. Tío Lalo let out a super loud breath, and Abuelita covered her face and cried.

"I have presents for everyone," Tío Lalo said. He looked at Papi. "Don't worry, I didn't steal anything. I sold my car."

Papi raised his eyebrows and tilted his head. I wondered who would buy that piece of junk and how much they paid for it. Maybe Papi wondered that too. But he didn't say anything.

"The teddy bear is for the baby." Tío Lalo handed the bear to Papi. "The flowers are for Mecho."

Abuelita jumped up and took the flowers from him. "I'll find something to put these in." She walked out the door.

Tío Lalo reached into the brown shopping bag and pulled out a box. "This is for you." He handed the box to Connie.

"A new Barbie!" Connie ran around the room and waved the box around. "Barbie! Barbie! Barbie!" She struggled to open the box. "Help me, Papi!"

Papi squatted down next to Connie. "All right, calm down," he said.

Tío Lalo had smaller boxes for the rest of us—jewelry. Mine was a necklace with red stones. "It's for you to wear to your concert with your new red dress," Tío Lalo said.

I looked at the necklace. It sure would match well with the dress Mami and Gracie had been making. But not with my new green dress. The necklace reminded me of something else, though: the headband Mami gave me for my birthday! I had forgotten all about it. What had Mami thought when I showed her my new green dress? Had she assumed I didn't care about her present because I didn't look for a dress to go with it? And the truth was that I had completely forgotten about the headband. I had been so excited about getting a new dress so I could play at the recital, I hadn't thought about anything else.

"Do you like it?" Tío Lalo asked.

"Oh, yes, it's beautiful." I gave my uncle a hug and looked over his shoulder at Mami. She was busy showing Gracie how to change Marisol's diaper. I hoped she wasn't upset that I wouldn't wear the headband to Lincoln Center. Even if she was, I knew she would forgive me. She always did.

Chapter 43

MAMI AND MARISOL WERE BACK HOME by Monday. Papi took the week off from work. He kept reminding Mami to take it easy, and he even cooked some Mami-style meals instead of just ordering pizza. But we did eat pizza once. Connie was all over the baby all the time. Gracie and I had to entertain her a lot so she could let poor little Mari sleep. But the baby wasn't really interested in sleeping when she had all of us to stare at. Mami put her in a little bouncy seat in the living room and she just watched us walking back and forth all the time. We never heard her cry at night. My sisters and I agreed that she was pretty much perfect. Of course, we weren't the ones changing her poopy diapers or getting up to nurse her in the middle of the night. Mami seemed a little tired during the day, but she smiled and hummed to herself, so I knew she was okay.

One day when I got home from school, Papi was sitting at the computer. "Come look at this email, Ana

María," he said. It was from the Eleanor School, and it was good news!

Congratulations! After reviewing the scholarship applications and test scores, we have selected five finalists for the prestigious Roosevelt Award, which will cover full tuition for one student. We are pleased to inform you that you are one of the finalists.

I read that last sentence over and over again, unable to breathe. Could this really be happening? I read on and saw that I now needed to complete the third step in the process. *We look forward to meeting you and your parents during your interview in January.*

"Congratulations," Papi said. I gave him a big hug, but I was speechless. "What's the matter?" he said. "Aren't you happy?"

"Yes!" I said. "But I'm kind of nervous. I mean, what if I mess this part up, after getting so close?"

Papi laughed. "You just love to worry, don't you? I'm sure the interview will be fine."

"I hope so," I said. "I should call Claudia. Maybe she'll have some pointers on how to prepare for the interview."

"I don't think you need to do anything to prepare," Papi said. "Just go in there and be yourself. Your intelligence and passion for learning will show, and they'll see that they'd be lucky to have you in their school." Then he turned back to his emails.

I thought about what Papi had said as I pulled out my piano books. Could he be right? Would the Eleanor School be impressed by plain old me? So far, it seemed that they had been. Maybe there was a good reason for that. Maybe they thought *they* needed to impress *me* at the interview. Did I feel confident enough to think that too?

* * *

The following Saturday, the mail carrier buzzed us and said we had a package. Papi went downstairs to get it and came back with a big pink box from Tía Nona. Mami put it on the coffee table and we gathered around to watch her open it.

"Aww!" we said when she lifted the first item out of the box. It was a tiny red velvet dress.

"Just like mine!" Connie said.

"Now you and your baby sister will match in your Christmas dresses," Mami said.

The teeny pink dress was adorable too. So were the shoes and socks, and the little T-shirt with the Dominican flag on it. "And here's something for you girls," Mami said. She took out four little jewelry boxes and handed them out. We all got earrings. Mine were red. They matched perfectly with the headband from Mami and the necklace from Tío Lalo. Why did everybody still think I was going to wear the red dress?

"Let's try on our earrings!" Gracie jumped up and ran to the bedroom with Rosie and Connie trailing after her.

I wasn't in a hurry to try mine on, so I stayed put.

"Oh, look, there's one more thing in here," Mami said. She took out a plastic container with a note taped on top. She peeled off the note and opened it. Her eyes moved across the page, then she handed me the container and the note.

Dear Anamay,

I remember how much you loved turrón when you ate it at my house, so I had the cook make you a batch. Enjoy!

Love,
Tia Nona

I opened the container and looked at the squares of crunchy coconut candy. They would taste delicious with a glass of cold milk. I counted eight pieces. If I ate them slowly, just one a day, I could stretch this out for over a week. My mouth watered thinking about it.

"See my pretty earrings!" Connie ran to Mami and stuck one ear in Mami's face, then the other. Rosie and Gracie were right behind her.

"Ooh, *turrón!*" Rosie peered into the container and licked her lips. "Is that for us?"

I looked at my sisters' eager faces. "Yes," I said, slipping the note under my bottom. "See, there's two pieces for each of us."

"Can I have one now, please?" Rosie clasped her hands.

"Yes, but only one," Mami said. "I don't want you to spoil your appetite."

My sisters ran to the kitchen to pour the milk. Mami gave me a grateful smile.

* * *

Sarita showed up at our house that afternoon. "I thought you might need help cleaning," she said.

"Thank you, Sarita," Mami said. "But that's not necessary."

"I don't mind," Sarita said. "And it's nice to get away from my little brothers for a while."

Mami laughed. "Well, you're always welcome to stop by and visit anytime. You don't have to clean."

Sarita and I cleaned up anyway while Mami napped with Connie and Mari. After we vacuumed, we sat down to rest on the sofa. I stared at the piano across the room. My piece still didn't sound as good as I wanted it to. "Hey, Sarita, could you help me with something?" I said.

"Sure, what's up?"

"Well, I just can't get my recital piece right, and I'm wondering if you can give me any pointers."

"Okay, let me hear it."

I played "Meine Freuden" while Sarita stood beside me and listened.

"Hmm," she said. "Technically, it's perfect. But what do you feel when you play it?"

I looked at Sarita. "I don't know. I'm just thinking about the notes and hoping I don't mess up."

"You just told me what you're thinking, not what you're feeling."

"Oh." I hadn't noticed that.

"What does 'Meine Freuden' mean?" Sarita asked.

I shrugged, then went to the computer and looked it up. "It means 'my joys,'" I said.

"Perfect!" Sarita said. "What gives you joy?"

"Um, I guess spending time with my friends," I said. "But . . . how will that help me play? Shouldn't I come up with some strategy to make sure I don't forget the notes?"

Sarita shook her head. "You won't forget the notes. Don't think about them anymore. Just feel the music. And feel the joy you get from your friends."

Even though I knew Sarita was right, "Meine Freuden" was really tough, and there would be a gazillion people watching me at the showcase. I was so afraid of making a mistake that my mind wouldn't let me stop worrying about the notes. But I hadn't thought about the notes when I played "Für Elise" at Tía Nona's house. I had been so worried about Clarisa that I had let the music into my heart as my fingers played what they already knew. And I had felt a little better after that, as if I had listened to a beautiful piece of music played by someone else. Could I perform "Meine Freuden" like that? I had to try. "Thanks for helping me," I said to Sarita. "Hey, do you want to see my dress for the recital?"

We went to my room and I pulled my new dress out of the closet.

Sarita held her hand out and rubbed the fabric between her fingers. "This is beautiful," she said. "But . . . is this what we're supposed to wear?"

"What do you mean?"

"Well, I was just going to wear the skirt I wore to graduation with a nice sweater."

I remembered Sarita's eighth-grade graduation skirt. "I don't think you can wear a jean skirt to Lincoln Center," I said.

"Oh." Sarita sat down on the bed. "Are you sure?"

"Well, maybe you should ask Doña Dulce. She'll know for sure."

"Okay."

"Maybe she'll say it's fine," I said. "I mean, what do I know? I've never been to one of these things."

Sarita smiled. "Yeah, maybe she'll like my outfit."

I didn't think so, but I didn't want to upset Sarita. Besides, it didn't matter what she wore. The audience would be mesmerized by her playing. I, on the other hand, needed to look good.

Chapter 44

I WAS RIGHT ON TIME TO MY last piano lesson before the Winter Showcase. When I stepped into Doña Dulce's house, I noticed something was different. It was quiet behind the front bedroom door. "Where's Sarita?" I asked Doña Dulce's husband. He shrugged, so I asked Doña Dulce.

Doña Dulce shook her head. "Sarita's not going to Lincoln Center."

"What?! Why not?"

"It turns out she doesn't have anything appropriate to wear. I wish she had told me sooner. Maybe I could have helped her find a dress." She sat forward in her seat. "All right, let's listen to your piece. It was good last week, so I'm sure you're ready."

I couldn't concentrate, but I played anyway, all the while thinking about Sarita. She was right that I shouldn't worry about the notes; I had played them so many times that my fingers just picked the right ones automatically. But the part about thinking of the things that brought me joy was a little trickier. Only Sarita came to mind, and I was filled with sad thoughts.

"Not bad," Doña Dulce said. "But you need to add more energy to it."

I played it again. I tried to be more upbeat, but it wasn't easy. I played it one more time, but the result was the same. I took my hands off the piano. "What if you bought a dress for Sarita, and she paid you back later?" I said.

"Ana María, I don't have that kind of money," Doña Dulce said. "And Sarita would never be able to pay me back. I already give her the lessons for free."

Oh. I did not know that. "Maybe she could go to Lincoln Center next year?" I said.

"I hope so," Doña Dulce said. "But her father wants her to get a job after school soon, so she might not play anymore."

"But she's so good!"

"I know. So much talent. It would be a shame to waste it." Doña Dulce stood up. "You're ready, so go enjoy the rest of the afternoon."

I stood up and gathered my books. I turned to Doña Dulce before I walked out. "What if Sarita gets a dress before Sunday?"

"That would be great. I already told her it's too late to change the program now, so as far as the Association is concerned, she's playing." Doña Dulce walked down the hall with me. "Let's keep our fingers crossed for her. If she finds a nice dress, all she has to do is show up."

I thought about Sarita as I walked home. This wasn't fair. It was bad enough that she couldn't live with her mother. Now she couldn't play at Lincoln Center either? And she was so good! She needed to play. And we needed to hear her play. How could I help Sarita? Would Papi buy her a dress if I asked him to? Maybe. But maybe not. And I really shouldn't ask. He'd already used the emergency credit card for my dress.

* * *

"Mami says we can wear our Christmas dresses to your recital," Rosie said at dinner. "Even little Mari."

"She's so cute." Connie said that every time anyone mentioned the baby, so everyone laughed. Except me.

"Are you nervous, *mamita*?" Mami reached over and put her hand over mine.

"I'm not going," I said.

"What?" Mami's hand stiffened.

I burst into tears. "My piece isn't good enough, so I can't go."

"What?!" Gracie stood up. "Did Doña Dulce say that?"

I stared at my plate. I didn't want to drag Doña Dulce into my lies.

"That witch! She doesn't know what she's talking about!" Gracie was getting worked up.

"Should I give her a call?" Papi said.

"No!" I looked at Papi. "It's fine, and it's true. I'm not ready to play at Lincoln Center. Maybe next year." I got up and ran to my room.

I sat in the dark and thought about what I had just said to my family. Was I making the right decision? Could I still get a full scholarship to the Eleanor School if I didn't play at Lincoln Center? Maybe I could play the piano for the admissions committee during my interview in January. Claudia said sometimes kids did stuff like that. Also, I knew my parents would make sure I got a good education one way or another. But Sarita didn't seem to have anyone to look out for her, and she could have a real future in music. Someone at Lincoln Center would surely notice her playing, and that could open doors for her. As her friend, I had to help her, and this was the only way.

* * *

My sisters didn't say anything to me the next morning as we got ready for school. They tiptoed around me like we had done with Gracie when she was grounded last summer. After breakfast Gracie and I went back to our room to get our backpacks. I went to the closet and took out my new green dress. I folded it carefully and put it in a bag. "What are you doing?" Gracie asked.

"I'm going to Sarita's house after school to give this to her," I said. "I don't need it now."

I thought Gracie would argue with me and tell me Sarita probably already had a dress, so what was I doing? She would say I could wear the dress another time. But Gracie didn't say anything. She just nodded, picked up her backpack, and walked out of the room.

* * *

I was glad Sarita wasn't home that afternoon. I handed the bag to Lucy when she opened the door. "Tell Sarita I had an extra dress, so she can have this one for Lincoln Center," I said.

Lucy's eyes opened wide. "Oh my goodness, she's going to be so happy! Thank you, thank you!"

"No problem," I said. "So, I'll see you at the Winter Showcase." I started to walk away, but then I turned and faced Lucy again. "Also, tell her I'm going to be really busy the rest of the week, so I won't have time to talk or anything. She doesn't have to call to thank me. We'll see each other at Lincoln Center." Then I ran down the steps, out the door, and all the way home.

Chapter 45

GRACIE DIDN'T GO TO SCHOOL THE next day. "I don't feel well, so Papi said he'd write me a note," she said at breakfast. She fake-coughed into her hand and went back to bed. I wondered if she was trying to get out of a test. More importantly, I wondered how she had managed to trick Mami and Papi into letting her stay home. But I didn't ask any questions. I didn't want her to get all snippety with me.

"Aren't you going to practice piano today?" Mami said when I got home from school.

"What for?"

Mami put her arms around me. "I know you're disappointed, *mija*, but you love to play. So you should practice to make yourself feel better."

She had a point. I sat at the piano and went through my whole routine. Scales. Arpeggios. Finger exercises. "Meine Freuden." I played my recital piece smoothly and cleanly. My rhythm was exactly as it should be, even the ritardando sections. And I didn't miss a single note. I was ready to perform at Lincoln Center, but now I would never get that chance. I could feel the Eleanor School slipping right through my fingers. When I finished playing, I noticed that my vision was blurred and my face was wet.

* * *

Gracie stayed home again the next day, which was weird because she had seemed fine at dinner the night before. Plus, it was Friday, and her teachers never gave tests on Fridays. So what was she avoiding? I really wanted to know. But I didn't ask. She probably wouldn't tell me anyway.

On Saturday morning Mami told me to take Rosie and Connie to the library. "It will take your mind off things," she said.

"It's *la pianista*!" Mrs. Rivera said when we walked in the door. She stood up and helped my sisters take off their coats. "Tomorrow's the big day, right?"

"Anamay's not going," Rosie said.

"Oh! Is that true?" Mrs. Rivera looked at me.

I nodded and looked away. "Are you doing story time now?" I asked.

Mrs. Rivera nodded. "Come on in, girls." Rosie and Connie followed her.

I walked over to the reference area. There was a half-done puzzle sprawled on the table. I sat down and searched for interlocking pieces.

"Don't you want to listen to the story today?"

I looked up and saw Ruben. I shook my head and turned back to the puzzle. He sat next to me. "What happened with the recital?" he said.

"I'm not going."

"I know, but why?"

"Why are you so nosy? You don't need to know everything, you know!"

Ruben stood up. "I was just asking. You don't have to bite my head off. I'm not the reason you're not going." He walked away.

Ruben was right. None of this was his fault. It wasn't anybody's fault. Except mine.

* * *

I went straight to my room when we got home from the library. Papi followed me in. "Ana María, we need to talk."

"I know, I know," I said. "Life isn't perfect and I need to learn to live with disappointment and all that." I flopped onto the floor and sat cross-legged.

Papi sat next to me. "Doña Dulce called the other day."

My heart thumped.

"She wanted to make sure we knew which entrance to use for the showcase."

I stared at my hands.

"It was very sweet of you to give your dress to Sarita.

Your mother and I are very proud of you. But you shouldn't have lied to us."

"I'm sorry," I said. "I know I shouldn't have lied, but I wanted to do this by myself, and if I had told you, you would have tried to help. But I should have told you, because I'm no good at this. You have nothing to be proud of."

"What are you talking about?"

"I thought I'd feel good about helping Sarita. I thought making a sacrifice for someone else would make me happy, the way I felt when I helped Clarisa. But I didn't give anything up for Clarisa, so it's not the same." I looked at Papi. "Now I'm so sad! And I'm mad too. I don't even know who I'm mad at!"

Papi put his arm around me, and I rested my head on his shoulder. "It's not easy to give up something important to you," he said. "But when you look back at this moment years from now, you'll feel happiness and pride."

I lifted my head and looked at Papi. "Do you ever feel sad about all that you've given up?"

"What have I given up?"

"You know, a job where you make a lot of money," I said.

Papi took a deep breath and looked off into space. "Well, sometimes I'm a little jealous of my former classmates, and Nona and Juan Miguel, and I wish I could give you girls more luxuries." He looked at me. "But the fact is that everything comes with a price. Remember when Claudia's grandfather died last year?"

"Yeah. Her dad had to go to work straight from his own father's funeral." Just thinking about it made me wince.

"When your mother and Rosalba were sick, my colleagues rallied and handled my cases for me, no questions asked. They value family just as much as I do. And at the end of each day, I feel good about all the clients I helped, and I'm glad to come home and spend time with my beautiful family. So your mother and I agree that, overall, the choices we've made have been good ones. I hope you feel that way about your choices too."

I thought about Claudia, and how she really didn't hang out with her parents that much because they had to work late all the time. They had made their choices, and they had to live with them. I had made a choice too when I gave my dress to Sarita. Was I happy with that choice?

Connie ran into the room and put her hands on my shoulders. "Don't cry, Anamay," she said.

I smiled and stuck two fingers under my glasses to wipe away the tears. "I'm okay," I said. And I meant it. I should have talked to my family sooner. "Can I go to the recital anyway?" I said to Papi. "I want to watch Sarita and cheer her on."

Before Papi could answer, Connie grabbed my hand and pulled. "Mami says come."

I stood up and followed Connie into the living room. Mami was on the couch nursing Marisol and smiling. Standing next to her was Gracie, holding up a dress.

My red dress. And it was finished. I stared at it, my mouth wide open. "Is this why you didn't go to school for two days?" I asked Gracie.

"Uh-huh. Now try it on, because I need to pin up the hem." She took me by the arm and led me to the bedroom. "You didn't give away your shoes, right?"

I shook my head.

"Good. Go get them."

I obeyed her. And then I let Gracie help me step into the dress. After I had the shoes on, I stood in front of the mirror while she got down on the floor with the pincushion next to her. "We weren't sure we'd get it done in time," Gracie said as she worked. "That's why we didn't say anything before. As it is, Mami will probably have to stay up late to hem it. And then we need to iron it in the morning." She stood up. "There! All done. Let's show Mami."

I couldn't take my eyes off the mirror. The dress was even more beautiful than I had imagined. The lace top had a sweetheart collar that left the perfect space for my new necklace. And the long skirt flowed and shimmered in the light.

"Anamay, why are you crying? I thought you'd be happy!"

"I am happy!"

Gracie laughed and took my hand. We went into the living room.

Chapter 46

WHEN THE ANNOUNCER CALLED MY NAME, I stepped onto the stage slowly. My heart pounded as I sat down and put my hands on the piano keys. When I pressed them and heard the sweet sound of the music, I stopped thinking about the notes. Instead, I thought about my friends and family. I started slowly and carefully, the way Ruben and I worked on our puzzles. I felt Claudia's cheerful energy as I sped up. My right hand glided across the keys like Mami's soothing voice, and the left hand joined in naturally and comfortably, like Papi's deeper voice combining with Mami's. As my fingers ran quickly along the keys, I could hear Connie's laughter, see Rosie twirl in her tutu, and feel Gracie's tight hugs. During a crescendo, I remembered my growing circle of family and friends—my new sister, all the relatives I had met in the Dominican Republic, Clarisa, and even Sarita. That circle would grow bigger if I went to the Eleanor School. But the scholarship didn't seem that important anymore.

Even if it didn't come through, I would be okay. I knew my family and friends would be there for me, always making sure I had what I needed and always bringing me joy. By the time I played the last note, I felt happy and relieved.

I put my hands on my lap and my whole body relaxed. I had played at Lincoln Center! And I had felt the music, like Doña Dulce and Sarita had said I should. Now all I had to do was get off the stage without tripping. I stood up and faced the audience. I bowed the way I had practiced at Doña Dulce's. My earrings from Tía Nona dangled when I bent my head down. I put my hand to my chest and felt Tío Lalo's necklace around my neck. I stood back up and held my head up high. For once, I knew my hair was perfectly in place. Abuelita had brushed and brushed it that morning, then twisted it up into a fancy bun held in place by a thousand bobby pins, and she put my new headband on like a tiara on a princess. And, of course, I was wearing the beautiful red dress Mami and Gracie had made for me, the dress Mami stayed up late to hem and Gracie got up early to iron.

I looked over at Doña Dulce. She waved her arms like she was pressing something down to the ground. She was telling me to take another bow. I turned back to face the audience. They were still clapping, even the other performers, who were sitting up front. Sarita was at the end of the row, since she would be playing last. She clapped loudly with her hands over her head. But the group in the third and fourth rows was going wild. I bowed again especially for them. Claudia waved at me and Ruben gave me two thumbs-up. My sisters and Chichi's girls were standing and shouting "Bravo!" Gracie put two fingers in her mouth and whistled loudly. Rosie pointed at me as she spoke enthusiastically with some strangers sitting in front of her. Then Connie joined in Rosie's conversation, jumping and pointing at me and then at herself. Even Tío Lalo was there, his arm around a teary Abuelita. She blinked and blinked as she cradled Marisol, who looked comfortable with her pink-and-white polka-dotted ear protectors. Papi had the camera up to his face. He was snapping away, and I could see his proud smile.

I laughed out loud when I saw Mami. Her head was on Papi's shoulder, and she was sound asleep. It was a good thing we had ordered the DVD.

Acknowledgments

Special thanks to:

Stacy Whitman for being an early and zealous advocate of this book;

Cheryl Klein for working tirelessly to provide me with pitch-perfect edits and insights, and helping me fine-tune the story;

Joyce Magnin for suffering through my entire first draft without complaint, and giving me wonderful advice and writing tips;

Marcia Everett for her upbeat answers to my many questions about sewing (and other things);

Laura Parnum, Amy Sisson, Nicole Wolverton, Glenn Benge, Jon Cohen, and Jon Miller, for reading early drafts and giving me great feedback;

All the generous writers I have met personally and online for selflessly sharing their knowledge and expertise, especially

Kell Andrews, who introduced me to "the Mayhem"; and

My family and friends for their majestic love, support, and encouragement, especially my daughter, Claudia, whose enthusiasm and IT assistance have been invaluable, and my son, Ruben, who should stop blaming himself for the many years between my completion of the first draft of this book and its publication — I made a choice to spend those years mothering (or smothering, as he would say) instead of writing, and I would gladly make that same choice again. Still, I thank him and his sister for growing up. Now I choose to write again, and the timing is perfect.